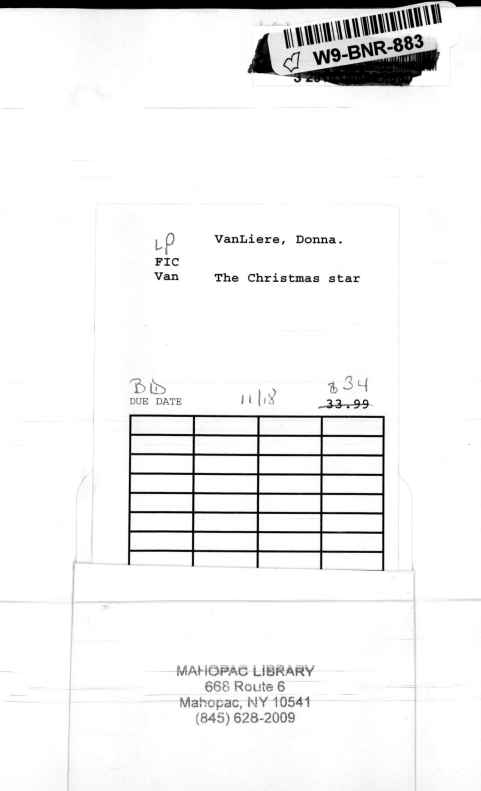

The Christmas Star

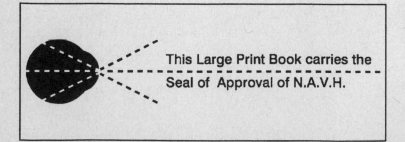

This Large Print Book carries the
Seal of Approval of N.A.V.H.

THE CHRISTMAS STAR

DONNA VANLIERE

THORNDIKE PRESS
A part of Gale, a Cengage Company

LP
FiL
VAN

Farmington Hills, Mich • San Francisco • New York • Waterville, Maine
Meriden, Conn • Mason, Ohio • Chicago

LIBRARY OF CONGRESS CIP DATA ON FILE.
CATALOGUING IN PUBLICATION FOR THIS BOOK
IS AVAILABLE FROM THE LIBRARY OF CONGRESS

ISBN-13: 978-1-4328-5791-2 (hardcover)

Published in 2018 by arrangement with Macmillan Publishing Group, LLC/St. Martin's Press

Printed in Mexico
1 2 3 4 5 6 7 22 21 20 19 18

*For Dannah Gresh,
who is a friend like Gloria
and Miriam to me*

ACKNOWLEDGMENTS

As always, many thanks to Jen Enderlin for your continued belief and enthusiasm, and to the entire marketing and sales department at St. Martin's Press. Much appreciation to Rachel Diebel for all your help.

I'm grateful to Joanna Kurtz, Jeff Dokkestul, and Melinda Mahand for your hearts.

And to Troy, Gracie, Kate, David, Lucy, CoCo, Katrina, and Cindy, who fill this house with joy, especially at Christmas!

You can't go back and make a new start, but you can start right now and make a brand-new ending.

— James R. Sherman

ONE

November 2011

Gabe Rodriguez opens an air return in the second-grade hallway and pulls out the filter. He has worked in the facilities and maintenance department of the Grandon Elementary School for the last six years, repairing everything from a broken window, wobbly desk leg, and faulty window air-conditioning unit, to painting hallways and classrooms, pulling out dead shrubs and trees, and fixing out-of-order plumbing in the school kitchen and every bathroom. It's a job that has kept him busy from morning until sometimes the early evening, but he doesn't mind the long hours. It keeps his mind occupied, driving away thoughts of another time and another life.

"Hi, Mr. G."

He turns from his work and sees seven-year-old Madeleine. "Good morning, Maddie. Are those new glasses?"

She shakes her head. "Nah. They probably just look new because I cleaned them today."

Gabe throws his head back and laughs. Sometimes these kids have no idea how funny they are. Maddie's right foot and leg were braced when she started kindergarten at Grandon and although she's now brace-free, her walk is gaited; she can't move as fast as other students. "Are you busting out of class?"

"No. I just need to get a book out of my backpack," she says, heading toward a locker. She opens her locker and tugs at the bright pink backpack, pulling it onto the floor. Her sandy-brown hair is up in pigtails and she's wearing a red Christmas sweatshirt with a snowman sporting a Santa hat on the front of it.

"You look awfully festive today," Gabe says, setting the old filter aside.

"We're doing presentations. I forgot my report," she says, pulling a paper from her backpack. "Mrs. Kurtz said if we look nice for our presentations that she'd give us extra points." She looks down at her shirt. "I don't know if this is nice enough."

He stops his work, smiling at her. "What?! Once you go to the front of the classroom Mrs. Kurtz is going to give you those points right away." He uses his hand and pretends to make checkmarks on it. "Does Maddie look nice? No doubt! She's picture-perfect!" She grins, hanging the backpack on the hook inside her locker. "What's your presentation on anyway?"

"Florence Nightingale."

"Is she the woman on the pool and hot tub commercials?"

She giggles. "No! She was the one who started nursing."

He grabs the new filter. "That's right! That was going to be my next guess."

She walks toward her classroom. "See you later, Mr. G."

"Tell me how you did!" He begins to put the new filter into the air return. "And if you have time I want to actually hear your speech about the gymnastic lady."

"She was a nurse!" Maddie says, shaking her head and opening the door to the classroom.

When he was young, Gabe worked with his dad mowing lawns and doing landscaping work, and because his dad felt insecure about his English, he acted as translator when they spoke to customers. His father moved to the States when he was twenty-six and fell in love with Molly, his English-as-a-second-language instructor, a fair-skinned

13

white girl from Alabama, with light brown hair, blue eyes, and a molasses-thick accent. Gabe and his sister are the first Rodriguezes to be born in the United States; most of the relatives on his dad's side of the family still live in Guatemala. While he has his mom's nose, his other features seem to have come from his dad: dark, wavy hair, and dark eyes and skin. Here at the elementary school he often finds himself speaking Spanish to several of the parents who also struggle with English. After years of working outside, Gabe thought he would go to college right out of high school and get a degree in business or finance. Growing up, he had watched his dad struggle to pay the bills, trying to find jobs as a landscaper throughout the winter, and knew he didn't want to be in landscaping forever. When this job at the elementary school opened up, he jumped on it, hoping his landscaping experience would help and it did. He never thought that when he was thirty-four he would still be in Grandon, but here he is. He closes the air return and makes his way down the hall to the next one.

At the end of the school day, Gabe lowers the American flag at the front of the building and folds it. Walking to the doors, he notices Maddie waiting on the sidewalk with

14

a few other children. "So how did it go?" he says, tucking the flag under his arm.

"I got a ninety-eight. I forgot to say when she died. But then I got extra points for being dressed nice and got a hundred."

"That's what I'm talking about!" He raises his hand and she high-fives him. The wind picks up and he pulls the hood of her jacket up over her head. "Do you have time to tell me about Miss Nightingale or is your van about to get here?"

She smiles. "It's always late so I have time. Do you want to hear the whole speech or just the highlights?"

"Whatever you want to give me."

Maddie crosses her arms against the cold and looks up at him. "Well, Florence Nightingale was born in 1820 in Italy and her parents wanted her to get married but she didn't want to be married. She wanted to be a nurse. So even though a man wanted to marry her, she didn't really want to marry him and studied to be a nurse. She was so good at it that she was asked to help lead nurses in the Crimean War and she made sure that the hospital was really clean and the patients were clean too. She'd walk from bed to bed holding a lamp and the soldiers called her the Lady with the Lamp. After the war she got a lot of awards and even some money for everything she did and she started a hospital and a training school for nurses." She shrugs, lifting her hands as if to say, *that's it.*

Gabe opens his eyes wide, looking at her. "That is the best presentation I've ever heard. And now I can say that I know all about Florence Nightingale and never think that she's the hot-tub lady ever again."

"You never did a presentation on Florence Nightingale?" Maddie asks. He shakes his head. "Have your kids ever done one?"

"I don't have any kids. Just all of you around here," he says, waving his arm toward all the other children. "All of you keep me really busy."

She folds her arms, looking at him. "Are you married?"

He shakes his head. "I was but I'm not anymore."

She squints as she stares at him, thinking. "You should be married. You'd make a good husband. I could find you a wife."

Laughter shakes him down to his work boots. "You know, I might just take you up on that. I could use all the help I can get."

She raises her finger high in the air. "Then I'm on it!"

"But what about you? Are you married?"

"No! Oh my gosh, Mr. G.! I'm too young!"

He smiles. "And there's no way your dad would want to give you away." Her face clouds over and Gabe attempts to explain. "You know, a dad often walks down the aisle with his daughter to give her away to her groom on her wedding day."

She's quiet as she looks at him. "I know. I've seen that in movies." She looks down at the ground and Gabe could kick himself. What a dumb thing to say!

"Here comes your ride," he says. A white van with the words GLORY'S PLACE, written on the side pulls to a stop in front of them. The driver jumps out of the van to mark each child's name off on the clipboard he's holding. "See you tomorrow. Congratulations again on your presentation."

"Bye, Mr. G."

He scolds himself for opening his big mouth as he walks back into the school. He is heading for the maintenance office when he sees Mrs. Kurtz at the end of the hall. He hesitates, wondering if he should speak to her but decides that he should. Mrs. Kurtz is one of the teachers in the school who has been there the longest and he has always seen her to be loving and kind toward her students. He pretends to be doing something with the flag as she approaches. "Did you have a good day, Mrs. Kurtz?"

"I did, Gabe! How was yours?"

"Good. Good. Maddie just did her presentation for me."

She stops in front of him. "It was so good. They all were just excellent today."

"Um . . . she . . . uh . . . asked if I was married and then I teased her, asking if she was married and she of course laughed and said no. And I said that there's no way her dad would want to give her away." He sighs. "I could tell by looking at her that I said the wrong thing." Mrs. Kurtz nods, understanding. "I never ask the kids about a mom or dad. I know that many of them live with a single parent or a grandparent. It just slipped out today." He shakes his head, feeling stupid. "I never would do or say anything to make her or any of these kids feel bad about —"

She interrupts him. "Many children here are in one-parent homes." She's careful how she phrases her words. "Some don't have either parent in their life." She looks at Gabe and he understands. "I can assure you that Maddie does not hold a grudge against you and that tomorrow she'll be the same happy little girl that she is every day." She smiles. "I have to run." She begins to hurry down the hall. "Haircut appointment and Loralei hates tardiness!"

He opens the door to the maintenance office and places the flag on its shelf. He grabs the tools he needs in order to put a leg back on a library table and sighs, shaking his head. There was a time, years ago, when something as simple as a slip of the tongue would not have bothered him. As a matter of fact, he gloried in his anger and temper and fiery tongue. But today he hates the thought that he has darkened a little girl's day.

Two

Lauren Gabriel drives through the town square, admiring the historic firehouse and the bank, and Betty's Bakery, which was originally the feed store back in the early 1900s. Some of the storefronts are already decorated for Christmas, with simple lights, evergreen swags, fake snow, or a wintry scene depicted in a store window. She's called Grandon home for a year, but by the way the townspeople adopted her as family, it feels as if all twenty-two years of her life have been spent here. Lauren stops at a red light and notices that a small group of people are decorating the three fir trees around the gazebo and the gazebo itself. The finishing touch seems to be a giant star on top of the gazebo. She cranes her neck to see it, realizing it wasn't there last year. She remembers everything about this gazebo and the town square and the moment she realized she was home, for the first time in her life. The star is high enough and big enough for the entire town to see. A young woman around her age and an older woman point up at the star, giving direction to the man on the roof of the gazebo. On closer look, she realizes that her boyfriend, Travis, is that man on top of the gazebo; he's hard at work with the Grandon Parks Department, and as Lauren pulls away from the light, she taps her horn, waving and yelling at him from the window.

Thirty-two-year-old Amy Denison tucks her blondish-brown bob behind her ears and cleans a smudge off her glasses as she looks at the sign on the door:

Glory's Place
A Place of Help and Hope

She opens it, stepping inside. The vestibule is filled with children, making their way to cubbies lined against the wall, in order to hang up their jackets and backpacks. Several adults greet them, leading them to games, to bookshelves lined with books, to tables where they begin homework, or to a doorway marked TUTORING. The place buzzes with activity and noise and Amy wonders if she is up for this, feeling inadequate. She had always assumed that she would have children of her own at this age but maybe this is as close as she will ever get.

"Are you Amy?"

An older woman with short salt-and-pepper curls is smiling at her. "I am. I'm here to see Gloria."

The woman's face lights up, and she moves toward Amy with open arms, hugging her. "That's me! So nice to meet you! Come on in." She leads her to a small office, pointing to a folding chair as she sits on one next to her. There's nothing fancy about this office but somehow Gloria makes it feel homey. Maybe it's her Southern accent or her warm smile, or maybe it's her open face that would delight anyone who walks through these doors that makes Amy feel instantly welcome. "We got all the background checks that we needed and you'll be happy to know that you are not wanted by the state or federal government."

"That is good to know!" Amy says, chuckling.

"I know you talked in depth with Heddy when you came in a few weeks ago but I always like to chat with volunteers before they begin. What brought you to Glory's Place?"

Amy lifts her shoulders. "I don't know if I

have a great answer for that, but I was at lunch one day thinking about what I would do that night, and what I would do that coming weekend, and I realized that my life pretty much revolves around myself. I've always liked children, I enjoy being with them, and the more I thought about my life the more I felt that I was supposed to be a foster parent. So I went through the training and all the paperwork. I'm just waiting for clearance with the state. I'm tired of the sameness of my life and thought that maybe you could use me here." For some reason Amy feels like crying and looks down at her purse before any tears form.

"We sure can use you and all of the kids will enjoy getting to know you." She glances down at her watch. "The van from Grandon Elementary will be here in just a couple of minutes and we can greet them together. You'll find that the volunteers do everything here. They greet the children, they help with homework, they play games with them, read to them, prepare snacks, help tutor them in a subject they're struggling with, help with the Christmas benefit, and clean the building. When I started this place many years ago with just a handful of friends we were doing the same things then that we are now." She laughs. "If you were looking for something glamorous then you've come to the wrong place!"

"I gave up dreams of glamour a long time ago," Amy says. She looks at Gloria, thinking. "Is the name on the door and your sign out front a misprint?"

Gloria shakes her head, smiling. "The kids call me Miss Glory. People have always called me Glory, with the exception of Miriam, who thinks Glory is a ridiculous name for a grown woman. You'll meet Miriam. I'll pray for you as you meet her. And you can call me whichever name is agreeable to you."

Amy looks up as a young Hispanic-looking woman with long dark hair and skin sticks her head inside the office door. "Excuse me, Glory?" Gloria turns in her seat. "Besides Trevor, did you want me to work with anyone else on math right away?"

Gloria jumps up. "Oh, Lauren! Come say hi to Amy. This is her first day."

Lauren steps forward to shake Amy's hand. "Hi! Glad you're here!"

Gloria puts her hand on Lauren's shoulder. "Lauren came last year to help us with our fund-raiser and decided not to leave." Lauren shrugs, smiling. "She moved to Grandon and became a florist at Clauson's Supermarket, has a handsome beau at the parks department, and is like a big sister to a lot of the kids here."

"Great to meet you," Amy says.

"Just ask me if you need anything," Lauren says.

Gloria claps her hands together, thinking. "Now! Besides Trevor, take Ally as well. I think those two will work well together without being distractions to each other. After them, could you take Derek and Logan? Their teachers have said they're still not grasping division."

"Got it!" Gloria and Amy can hear Lauren calling for the first two boys as she exits the office.

"Are you working today, Gloria? Or is your day going to be filled with tea and crumpets?"

Gloria shakes her head and, without looking, points her thumb over her shoulder. "That is Miriam."

Amy shakes her hand. "I'm Amy. A new volunteer."

"Oh, how wonderful," Miriam says, looking her over. "What do you do, Amy?"

"I'm an insurance adjuster."

Miriam scrunches up her face. "Oh my! That does sound terribly dull, doesn't it?" Amy is taken off guard and laughs. Miriam's English accent is so smooth and gentle that she can't tell if her comment was meant to be insulting or not. "Are you married?"

"No, I'm not."

"Children?"

Amy shakes her head. "No. But I love children. That's why I'm here."

"Where do you live?"

"In Cortland."

Miriam raises her eyebrows. "That's a thirty-minute drive! I wonder if you could have found any volunteer opportunities closer to your front door?"

Gloria steps forward, putting her hand on Amy's back. "I forgot! I need to show you the big room!" She leans in, whispering, "I'm rescuing you from Miriam," and leads her into the vestibule, pointing across the room filled with children. "We call this 'the big room.' Just go right across the big room and bring your purse and jacket through that door," she says, pointing. "Just pick any empty locker and I'll meet you right back here to greet the van."

When she is out of earshot, Gloria turns back to Miriam and says, "I keep hoping that one day you will learn some tact, but it appears that as you are getting elderly and more infirm, you are losing tact altogether."

Miriam looks shocked. "Whatever did I say?"

"You said her job was boring and you asked if she was married or had children!"

"I was getting to know her. My parents always called that being polite and inquisitive."

Gloria sighs. "Her application reveals that she is not married and does not have any children. How do we know that's not a wound for her?"

Miriam rolls her eyes. "Everything is a wound these days."

"You're my wound," Gloria says, whispering.

"I heard that, Gloria," Miriam hisses, heading toward the tutoring room.

Gloria waves when she sees Amy walking toward them, and heads to the front door so she'll follow behind. "Now you've met Miriam! I'm sorry to say that she'll never improve beyond what you saw today."

Amy laughs. "I like her!"

Gloria nods her head. "Me too, but don't tell her that!" At the sight of the van on the street, Gloria opens the door, stepping out onto the sidewalk. "Ten children come to us each day from the elementary school. The school has its own after-school program but our program lasts longer."

"What time do parents pick up their kids here?" Amy asks, watching the van pull in to the driveway.

"The last of the children leave around seven thirty."

"Wow! That's a really long day for kids."

Gloria nods, looking at her. "That's why we try to give these kids structure and encouragement and love. We know that this is the closest thing to a home that many of these kids have right now." She waves as the van pulls to a stop, opening the side door. "Here are my favorite kids!"

"You say that every day, Miss Glory," a small boy with blond, messy hair says, jumping out onto the sidewalk.

"I speak the truth, Jace," she says, tapping him on top of the head. "Say hello to Miss Denison. She's new here." Jace waves as he runs into the building. "Everybody say hello to Miss Denison when you get out of the van," Gloria says, hugging the shoulders of each child as they step out. She reaches her hand inside the van and helps the final little girl out. "How are you today, Miss Madeleine Grace?" She turns to look at Amy. "Madeleine means 'high tower' and Grace means 'God's favor,' and as you can see Miss Maddie is the perfect picture of a high tower of God's favor!"

"I can see that!" Amy says, taking Gloria's lead. "I love your glasses, Maddie."

Maddie looks up at Amy. "I like your glasses too! I always wanted a pair of blue ones like that but mine are just brown."

Amy bends over, adjusting the glasses on Maddie's face. "Brown and very stylish."

"You're new here. I've never seen you before."

Gloria closes the van door, turning to them. "Maddie! I just had the best idea! Miss Denison just arrived and I need to take her around and show her everything. Do you think you could do that for me?"

Maddie nods and lifts her backpack over her shoulder. "Sure! Just follow me."

Amy follows her to a bank of cubbies, where Maddie hangs her jacket and backpack. "These are the cubbies where we keep our stuff. We aren't allowed to put anything on the floor because it gets messy with so many kids." Amy smiles at how grown-up Maddie sounds. Maddie hurries to a section of tables by the front windows. "This is where we can play games. We pick a game from here," she says, pointing to shelves behind the tables. "And when we're done with it, we have to put it away. Miss Glory says this is like our house and we have to keep it tidy."

"Those are good rules," Amy says, following after her.

"We can find a book here and use the beanbag chairs or sit at a table or just on the floor to read. I don't like sitting on the floor."

Amy noticed Maddie's walk and assumes it is too hard to get up and down off the floor for her. "I don't like the floor either. It's too hard and it's difficult to get up off it too."

Maddie looks at her, surprised. "Really? Maybe it's because you're old."

Amy throws her head back, giggling. "It probably is! Why don't you like to sit on the floor?"

"Because a bug with long legs and wings crawled on my leg one day and he wouldn't have done that if I was sitting on a beanbag chair."

Amy leans over, whispering. "Does this place have a bug problem? Because I hate bugs!"

Maddie shakes her head and takes Amy by the hand, leading her across the room. "No. Dalton said he's never been able to hear right since I screamed that day and he took care of the bug problem. That's Dalton over there," she says, pointing to an African-American man with gray hair, jumping rope with two girls. "That's where we can be active. There are jump ropes and basketballs and other stuff that we can use. I don't go to that side of the big room, except when Dalton makes me dance with him." She leads Amy toward the door marked TUTOR-ING.

"Don't you like dancing with Dalton? He looks like he'd be a great dancer."

"Dalton's the best dancer and I'm the worst."

Amy stops before Maddie opens the door to Tutoring. "I'm not a good dancer either but I have fun doing it."

"You have fun because your legs are normal," Maddie says, grinning.

Amy bends toward her. "There's something wrong with your legs?"

"Just this one," she says, tapping her right thigh. "Everybody knows it's CP." Amy doesn't respond. "Cerebral palsy. I've had it since I was little. I don't like it because it makes me walk funny and it's the first thing people see."

"It wasn't the first thing I saw. I saw your beautiful face and glasses and your awesome smile and was struck by your amazing name! Madeleine Grace. So beautiful."

The little girl twists the doorknob in front of her. "My parents don't know me. A nurse named me that."

Amy's heart sinks as she follows her into the room.

THREE

Twenty-five-year-old Travis Mabrey walks into Glory's Place at seven, wearing jeans, a flannel shirt, and Carhartt jacket. Travis works for the Grandon Parks and Recreation Department and his job brought Lauren into his life one year ago this month. On the evenings that she closes, he arrives to help clean as she gets the last of the children loaded into cars. Travis spends his days keeping ball fields in shape and city parks looking beautiful, so he doesn't mind sweeping and mopping floors; sanitizing tables, toys, and games; emptying trash cans; or cleaning windows at Glory's Place. He enjoys the children and when he and Lauren are finished, they are always hungry and ready for dinner.

"Hi, Mr. T.," Maddie says, waving as he comes in the door.

"Maddie!" Travis says, giving her a high five. "How's school?"

"Good! I rocked a Florence Nightingale presentation today."

Travis looks impressed. "Awesome!" He catches Lauren's eye and smiles. "Hi, babe!" She rolls her eyes, embarrassed.

"We all know he's your boyfriend," Maddie says, making the remaining three children laugh.

"Yeah," says Marcus, a ten-year-old with shaggy brown hair and a toothy smile. "We all know that you kiss each other when we're not around." The children begin to giggle as Lauren covers her ears.

"You looooove each other," Brianna says, her bright red hair bouncing in pigtails on each side of her head.

"Hey!" Maddie says, her hand on her hip. "You two should get married!"

Travis opens his mouth, pretending to be shocked, as the children begin to howl with laughter.

"Yeah," Brianna says. "When are you going to get married?"

"She doesn't have to get married," Luke says, running to stand near Lauren. "Maybe she wants to be with us instead." Lauren smiles, putting her hand on his shoulder and pulling him to her.

Travis nods, thinking. "I'm pretty sure that if she married somebody, she would still want to be with you."

Luke looks up at her. "Is that true?"

Lauren smiles. "Absolutely! What could ever tear me away from you guys?"

"A honeymoon," Travis says, grinning.

"She can't go on a honeymoon!" Marcus says, taking his place next to Lauren. "What's a honeymoon?"

Lauren bends over, laughing. "It's like a vacation that a newlywed couple goes on together."

"Just the two people together?" Luke asks. Lauren nods. Luke shakes his head. "Sounds boring. If you two get married, then you have to take us on your vacation with you."

Travis laughs, picking chairs up off the floor and setting them on top of tables. "Apparently, you guys don't know too much about honeymoons."

"And you don't know anything about Super Mario," Brianna says.

Travis retrieves the large broom from the storage closet and begins sweeping the floor. "You got me there!" he says, winking at Lauren.

The children help straighten books and wipe off games with cleaning wipes. Lauren feels especially close to these four children who are the last to be picked up each day.

Brianna's mom pulls into the driveway, followed by Luke's, and Lauren makes sure that they each have their jackets on before reaching for their backpacks. She hugs each child before sending him or her outside and notices Marcus's grandmother sitting in her car at the streetlight.

"Marcus! Grab your jacket and backpack." He races for his things and rushes for the door. She stops him, making sure his jacket is on. "See you tomorrow, handsome man."

He points to Travis with his thumb. "You better not let him hear you calling me that."

"I'm used to it!" Travis says, sweeping into a dustpan.

Lauren closes and locks the front door and watches as Maddie straightens the games on the shelves. She is always the last to be picked up. "So! Miss Denison seems great," Lauren says, organizing a shelf.

Maddie nods. "I like her! I like everybody here."

"Me too. I liked everybody at Glory's Place so much that I decided to move to Grandon. They were like family to me."

Maddie stops her work, looking at her. "Is that why you live with Miss Stacy and her family?"

"Yeah, it is. Stacy was the first person I met in Grandon, and because of her work here I got to meet Miss Glory and Miriam and Dalton and Heddy and all of you. After that, I just couldn't go anywhere else. I had to live here."

"But where's your real family?"

Lauren smiles. "This is my real family." She sits on the table. "If you mean where is the woman who gave birth to me or the man who is supposed to be my father, well, that's a great question. The truth is, neither one of them was cut out for being a parent. My dad left early on and my mom actually spent time in jail. When she got out she knew she couldn't raise me so I grew up in foster homes."

Maddie's face opens up. "I live in a foster home."

Lauren's eyes are full, seeing herself as a child in Maddie. She has wondered about Maddie's background because she never mentions a mom or dad, but Lauren can tell that her foster mom takes exceptional care of her. "You know what I always wondered about?" Maddie shakes her head. "I wondered what my dad looked like. I mean, I knew I must have looked like him because I didn't look like my mom. She had light skin and blondish-brown hair and I have dark skin and black hair. Of course I always wanted blond hair and light skin."

"I love your skin and hair," Maddie says, touching Lauren's ponytail.

"I love it, too. I wish I had loved it when I was your age."

Maddie is quiet, putting her hands in her lap. "I wonder what my mom and dad look like."

Lauren crosses her arms, looking at her. "Well, they might have this beautiful hair," she says, touching it. "Or maybe blue eyes, but all of it: the smile, the beautiful skin, the personality, the brains, all that is God's own special recipe to make you you."

"The cerebral palsy?"

"I know you don't think that it makes you beautiful but it does." Lauren bumps her forehead to Maddie's. A car turns in to the driveway and Lauren uses a British accent to say, "Your ride is here, milady!" She helps Maddie with her jacket and carries her backpack outside, opening the back door of the car, looking at Linda, her foster mom, who often works late as a nurse. "She had a really good day!" Lauren says. She sets the backpack at Maddie's feet. "See you tomorrow, beautiful!" She watches the car drive away and walks back into Glory's Place, locking the door behind her. She turns to see that Travis is waiting for her and her eyes fill with tears.

He moves to her, pulling her close. "She's one of your favorites, I know."

Lauren nods, wiping her face. "I see me at that age, you know?"

He takes her by the hand, leading her to the beanbag chairs. He sits down and pulls her onto his lap. "But with a huge difference." She looks at him. "You didn't have a Lauren at that age. You didn't have a Miss Glory or Glory's Place or any of these people at that age."

She rests her head on his chest and they sit in the quiet together. Lauren has always felt whole with Travis. She has never had to pretend to be anyone but herself with him. He is safe and kind and good, with simple tastes like hers.

"So what about it?" he asks, breaking into her thoughts.

"About what?"

"About what Maddie asked. When are we going to get married?"

She looks deflated. "We've talked about this. When we have money saved and we're on our feet."

He pushes her off his lap and stands. "We're on our feet."

She shakes her head, putting the broom and dustpan back into the closet. "You know what I mean. We need to save a lot more money if we want to get into a house." She shuts the door and turns. "We need to . . ." She stops talking when she sees that Travis is down on one knee.

"We need to what? Love each other more? That's not possible for me." Her eyes fill with tears again. "I loved you the day I met you in this place. You know that." Tears fall down her cheeks and she laughs. "If you're saying that we have to have a certain amount of money in the bank before we get married then that's never going to happen because life happens. But I don't want it to keep happening without you. I don't have a ring because I didn't plan this but . . ." She laughs out loud, wiping her face with her hands. "Lauren Gabriel . . . will you marry me?"

She crumbles in front of him, laughing and kissing him. "Of course I will!"

"Will you go on a honeymoon with just me or do we have to take all these kids with us?"

She laughs out loud. "Just you."

FOUR

Gabe has spent most of the morning in the school's kitchen fixing a leak under the dishwasher. He got to the school early, hoping to get the leak fixed before the breakfast dishes were ready to be cleaned. As with most projects, however, he had to make an unexpected trip to the hardware store for supplies. With just a few more adjustments, he will have everything back in place and the dishwasher ready for lunch. As he exits the cafeteria doors, he waits for two classes to pass before he heads toward the maintenance office.

"Hi, Mr. G.," many of the children say, waving as they walk by. Gabe smiles and says hello. When he first applied for this job, he thought the worst part of it would be dealing with children, but they have ended up being the best part of his work. They make him laugh, they always speak to him, on Valentine's Day they give him chocolates

41

and at Christmas they bring him cookies, and he always feels useful. He's grateful for this work and for this place. There are many times he wishes that a few years ago he could have been the person that he is today. Life would be different in so many ways; but he's learned that no matter how hard he tries, he can't change the past.

"Hi, Mr. G.," Maddie says, grinning. She stops and looks at him.

"Good morning, Maddie."

She lifts her little finger, pointing it at him. "I found a nice lady for you to date."

He throws his head back, laughing. "Oh wow! You were serious! Is this what you do? You set people up? Do you have a business card?"

She begins to walk in order to keep up with her class. "You're not married and she's not married and she's pretty." She looks at him over her shoulder. "I'll tell you more about her later."

"Set up by a seven-year-old. What could possibly go wrong?" he says, heading to his office.

Gabe is late retrieving the flag from the pole this afternoon. When he walks out the front door, he notices that the children who wait for the van from Glory's Place are already gone. He takes down the flag and folds it, before picking up some scraps of paper along the sidewalk and throwing them away. He pushes the door open as Maddie is about to pull it open on the other side. He looks at her, surprised. "Maddie! Are you going to Glory's Place?"

"Of course I am," she says, heading past him.

"Uh, I think the van has already left."

She looks frightened, quickening her pace to the end of the sidewalk. "No! No! I can't miss the van!" She begins to cry and Gabe runs to her.

He puts his hand around her shoulder. "It's okay. Let's go talk to Mrs. Kemper or someone else in the office and see how we can get you over there."

"I didn't think I would be late." She is crying harder and Gabe squeezes her shoulder. "I stopped to go to the bathroom. I never should've done that. I'm so slow!"

He kneels down in front of her. "You shouldn't have gone to the bathroom?" She shakes her head, tears welling in her eyes again. "You told me some things about Florence Nightingale that I didn't know. Now I'm going to tell you some things that apparently you don't know. Everybody is late at one time or another for something in their life and everybody has to go to the bathroom." She begins to smile. "This might really blow your mind but everybody inside the school today has gone to the bathroom. Trust me, I know!" She begins to laugh and he stands, patting her on the shoulder. "All right, let's find out how to get you to Glory's Place."

Mrs. Kemper is behind the counter in the office, talking with the school nurse when she glances up at the opening door. "Maddie? Are you hurt?"

"She goes to Glory's Place after school," Gabe says.

A look of realization crosses Mrs. Kemper's face. "And that van already left." She purses her lips and then mumbles, "How in the world did that driver leave a student behind?" Gabe can't tell if she's frustrated or angry or maybe both.

"I didn't mean to do it," Maddie begins to confess. "I had to go to the bathroom."

Mrs. Kemper smiles, looking over the countertop at her. "Well, that is not a big deal at all. Everybody has to go to the bathroom." Maddie looks up at Gabe and he smiles, shrugging as if to say, *I told you so.* "Maddie, I would be happy to get you over to Glory's Place."

Maddie peeks over the counter at Mrs.

Kemper. "You can drive me there?"

Mrs. Kemper nods. "I have my driver's license and everything."

Maddie looks at Gabe and then at Mrs. Kemper. "Can Mr. G. drive me there?"

Mrs. Kemper looks surprised. "Well, I . . ." She glances at Gabe. "Is this something that you could do, Gabe?"

He peers down at Maddie. "Sure!"

Mrs. Kemper begins riffling through files on her computer. "I will need to print out a transportation waiver that you'll need to take with you. It will be proof that this is a secondary means of transportation in order for Maddie to get to Glory's Place." She clicks print and they can hear the printer working behind her. She stands up and snatches it from the printer, grabbing a pen lying nearby. "Gabe, fill out this information about your vehicle."

He sets the flag on top of the counter. "Could you put this under the counter for me? I'll put it away when I get back."

As he fills out the waiver Mrs. Kemper asks, "Is your vehicle insured?" He nods. "And your insurance information is inside?" He nods, pushing the paper toward her. "It is. It's a safe, good truck."

"All right," she says, taking the waiver. She logs the information into her computer before signing the waiver and handing it back to Gabe. "Thanks so much for helping out. And Maddie, we'll see you tomorrow."

Maddie smiles and takes hold of Gabe's hand as they leave the office.

They walk down the sidewalk, heading to the staff parking lot. "Thanks for taking me, Mr. G."

"You're welcome," he says, taking her backpack from her. He fishes his keys out of his pocket and holds the fob in the air, unlocking a blue Ford truck.

"This is your truck?"

"It is," he says, opening the back door for her.

"This is really nice."

"Thanks! It's eleven years old and doesn't have any bells or whistles but you're right, it is nice."

She puts her seat belt on and looks over the seat at him as he slides behind the wheel. "Now I can tell you all about Miss Jenson."

He puts the key into the ignition. "Who?" Then he looks at her. "Oh! The woman that you said . . ."

"That you should go out with."

He grins as he looks in the rearview mirror to back up. "Did you miss the van on purpose? Just so you could tell me about . . .

46

What's her name?"

"Miss Jenson. She's brand-new at Glory's Place and is really sweet and really pretty, with glasses. She's also single. She told me."

He shakes his head. "She told you, or did you coerce the information out of her?"

She lifts her shoulders. "I don't know what that means. But she looks around your age."

He glances back at her. "I hate to ask but how old do you think I am?"

She studies him. "Fifty."

He slaps the steering wheel, laughing. "And you think she looks fifty?"

She nods. "She looks your age, so yeah! She's single and nice and you are single and nice and I'm going to tell her about you too."

He holds his hand in the air. "Hold on! You're killing me here! This typically isn't how people meet. Through some sort of seven-year-old matchmaker."

She crosses her arms. "You said you were married but you're not anymore. How did you meet your wife?"

He looks over his shoulder, checking the front of her coat. "Just seeing if you're wearing a journalist badge. My dad and I had done work for the company that she worked for and we were invited to their annual Christmas party. She was there and I thought she was cute and started talking to her." He stops at a red light and can feel her looking at him. "What now?"

"How long were you married?"

"Four years."

"Why aren't you married anymore?"

The light turns green and he begins to drive again, glancing over his shoulder. "The truth?" She nods. "I wasn't a good husband."

"You mean you were a bad husband?"

"Yeah, that's what I mean."

She shakes her head. "I don't think that's true."

He nods. "It is. You could ask my ex-wife. She would agree with me."

Maddie looks out the window and then back at Gabe. "How were you a bad husband?"

"I had a bad temper. I was angry a lot. I said things that a man shouldn't say to his wife and was just a jerk all the way around."

"I don't think you're like that anymore."

"I don't think I am either."

"People change." She says it with such finality that it makes him laugh.

He agrees, slapping the steering wheel for emphasis. "They can and sometimes they do change!"

"Maybe your ex-wife would like you again now."

He smiles. "My ex-wife has moved on."

"She moved away?"

"Yeah, she did, but what I mean is that she moved on with her life. New relationship and all that. Engaged. Maybe married by now. Not sure."

Maddie smacks her hands down on her thighs. "Well, then that means you definitely need to meet Miss Jenson." He drives around the town square and Maddie points out the window. "Look at that star on top of the gazebo! That's new!"

He looks up at it through the windshield. "Yep. That's new this year."

Her face is glued to the window as they approach the gazebo and star. "That's a sign."

"For what?"

"A star led the Wise Men to Jesus."

He chuckles, driving past the gazebo. "I'm aware of the story."

Her face falls flat as she looks at him. "All I'm saying is be wise and keep your eyes open. That star is a sign for you and Miss Jenson."

Gabe shakes his head and reaches behind him, squeezing her ankle. He pulls in to the driveway for Glory's Place and parks in front of the entrance. He gets out and runs to the other side, opening Maddie's door before getting her backpack off the backseat.

"One more thing about Miss Jenson," she says.

He holds up his hand. "I appreciate your efforts to help me but I —"

"Have moved on?" she says, looking at him. He can't answer that, not truthfully, anyway. "Can you just walk inside with me so that I can point her out to you?"

Gabe realizes that she will never take no for an answer and sighs, waving his arm in front of him for her to lead the way.

"Maddie!" Heddy says, swooping to her side. "I thought maybe you were sick today."

Maddie shakes her head. "I missed the van. But Mr. G. brought me."

Heddy extends her hand to shake his. "I'm Heddy. Thanks so much for bringing her. If that ever happens again you can call us here and we will come pick her up."

"Is Miss Jenson here yet?" Maddie says, craning her neck to scan the big room.

"Who?" Heddy says, shaking her head. "I don't think there's anyone here who . . . it's just me and Dalton, Gloria and Miriam right now."

Gabe exhales, relieved that this experiment has ended. "I'll see you tomorrow,

Maddie."

She wraps her arms around his middle, hugging him. "I think once you see her you'll want to stop moving on."

He pats her shoulder and heads through the front door for his truck. There is no way to stop something that has never started in the first place. He drives away from the entrance as Amy pulls in to a parking space.

FIVE

"You just missed Mr. G.," Maddie says, as Amy takes off her jacket.

"Who?"

"Mr. G.," Maddie says, following her through the door of a room where she hangs her jacket and purse inside a locker. "He dropped me off today and he's single like you."

Amy snaps her head as if she's being hit at every angle. "This is only my second day here. Will you be bringing in a minister to marry me and Mr. Wonderful on my third day?"

Maddie shrugs. "If I have to."

They hear Gloria raising her voice so that she can be heard in the big room, and Amy opens the door, leading Maddie out.

"We are just days away from the fund-raiser," Gloria says. "The choir sounds beautiful!" She spreads her arms out in front of the children. "I am so proud of all of you. Let's listen to Stacy and Lauren to see how they'd like to practice with you today. Lauren?"

Lauren steps into the middle of the children, folding her hands in front of her. "We will be separating you into smaller groups to work on some minor issues with each song, but before Stacy and I do that, I wanted to let you know that . . ." She looks around at their faces. "Travis and I are engaged!" The room erupts in gasps, clapping, laughter, and cheers.

"When did this happen?" Gloria says, hugging her.

Dalton and Heddy Gregory are next in line for hugs. They have been a huge part of Lauren's life at Glory's Place for the last year. "We couldn't be happier," Dalton says, squeezing her. Lauren tears up as he kisses her on top of her head. This wonderful man with his gentle, easy ways feels more like a dad than anyone she's ever known.

"Where is the engagement ring?" Miriam says, grabbing Lauren's hand to look at her empty finger.

"I don't have it yet, Miriam. It all happened so fast that Travis wasn't prepared."

Miriam makes a groaning noise inside her throat and rolls her eyes. "One should always be prepared. Especially with diamonds!"

"Would you keep your big nose out of their business," Gloria snaps. She smiles at Lauren. "Now tell us all about it."

Maddie grabs Amy's hand. "I did that! Last night I told them they should get married and now they're going to do it!"

"And that was because of you?" Amy says.

"Of course it was! That's why you should listen to me and meet Mr. G."

"Stacy, did you already know about this?" Gloria says.

Stacy smiles. "She lives with us. When she and Travis walk through our front door beaming, you have to know that something's up."

"And when will you get married?" Gloria asks.

"We don't know," Lauren says.

"There's so much to do to prepare!" Miriam says, clapping her hands together.

Gloria slaps her head. "Run! Elope now before Miriam becomes the most unwanted wedding planner in America."

Lauren knows that she doesn't need a fancy dress, a cake, or a ring to make a wedding. All she needs and wants is Travis and these people gathered around her.

When Gabe reaches the front of Clauson's

he heads for the shortest line, before realizing that the longer line is for the bagger who puts a note into a bag for each customer. Gabe has received a few notes over the last year and figures why not, stepping out of the short line into the longer one. Gabe doesn't know anything about the bagger, a young man around nineteen or twenty, he assumes, but by the length of the line each time this young man is bagging, he knows there must be something special about him. He takes his place in line and watches as the bagger shuffles through a stack of notes in his hands before inserting one into a bag for each customer, with notes like:

Christmas came as LOVE in a manger! Merry Christmas, Ben

If we let it, Christmas will lead us home. Hope you'll be home for Christmas! Love, Ben

You are someone's best gift this Christmas! Happy Christmas, Ben

"There's a shorter line over here if anyone would like to step over," the manager says, smiling at those in the longer line.

"We're fine, Les," an older woman says. "You suggest that every time and every time someone tells you that we're not moving. We want our note from Ben!"

"It's my job to make sure the customers are taken care of," the manager says, smiling.

"We're fine right where we are," the woman replies.

The manager chuckles and straightens up the candy bars and gum at the entrance to one of the lines.

Ben riffles through his notes and finds the perfect one for the woman in front of Gabe: *Grandmas are gingerbread cookies, chocolate fudge, and spicy nuts all rolled into one and the best memory of Christmas! Love, Ben.*

"I love it, Ben!" the woman says, patting his arm. "And I'll bring in some fudge on my next trip!"

Gabe watches Ben as he puts his groceries on the conveyor belt. "I haven't seen you in a long time," Ben says.

Gabe is impressed by his memory. "I don't get here very often. It's easier to go to a grocery store on the other side of town."

"That's okay," Ben says. "We understand. We like all the grocery stores in town."

Gabe pays and reaches for his bags, looking closely at the bagger's name tag to make sure he heard his name right. "Thanks, Ben."

"Have a great day," Ben says, busy with the next customer's groceries.

Walking toward the doors, Gabe reaches inside one of the bags and pulls out a small, square note. *Stars seem to shine brighter at Christmas. I hope you see how beautiful the stars are in your life. Merry Christmas, Ben.*

Gabe smiles and slips the note into his back pocket.

Gabe sits at a bench table inside Betty's Bakery and waves when he sees Travis walk through the door. He stands and gives him a hug before pointing out the window. "I like the star on top of the gazebo. Parks and Rec is really stepping up the decorations."

"We put it up but it's not ours," Travis says. "A woman and her kids bought it and wanted it put up right away."

"Who was the dope who got roped into climbing up there with a star on his back?"

"That dope would be me!" Travis says, sitting opposite him.

Gabe laughs. "Excellent work. Better you than me." He reaches for his coffee cup. "What's so important that you can't leave a message?"

Travis rests his hands on the table, smiling. "I was just wondering if you'd be my best man?"

Gabe's eyes widen. He extends his hand, shaking Travis's. "You did it!"

Travis nods. "Last night. I didn't plan on it. It just happened. So . . . will you?"

"You know I will! You are my favorite cousin! When's the day?"

Travis shrugs. "Not sure yet. I say the sooner the better."

Gabe laughs. "I'm sure you do! I'm happy for you. Lauren's great. I dropped a student off at Glory's Place today and kind of looked for her but I didn't see her. I was trying to get out of there as fast as possible."

"Why?"

He shakes his head, smiling. "A little girl at school is trying to set me up with some new woman who works there. Do you know her?"

"No. But by the time I get there each day everybody has left except for Lauren and a few kids who are there for late pickup. But I'll keep my eyes open and let you know what she looks like."

Gabe grins. "You are off the hook. Trust me, I'm not interested."

Travis looks at him. "Really? You got divorced, what, six years ago? You're not interested in getting back out there?"

Gabe sips his coffee. "I've been out there. I stink at it."

Travis nods. "What about the woman at AA?"

"We went out two times, like, eight months ago! As you know, my track record is less than stellar."

Travis chuckles. "Hey, I'm your family and I have to love you but I can agree that you were an idiot a few years ago."

"Thanks, man. I'm feeling the love."

Travis bangs the table. "You know what I mean. You were out of control. But you've cleaned yourself up. You're the guy that I knew before you started drinking."

Gabe looks around the restaurant, thinking. "You know . . . She never knew the real me. The night we met I was almost drunk and by the end of the party I was smashed. That's how she knew me."

"Yeah, well, the next woman will know the real you. You're sober for how long now?"

"Five and a half years."

"In five and a half years you've changed. You have a job that you love and you're taking college classes at night to become a teacher. You! A teacher!" Gabe nods, chuckling in agreement that it sounds absurd. "The old Gabe could never be a teacher but this Gabe, the real Gabe, can and *will be* a teacher! You're a good man and I bet the woman you meet will be a good woman."

"I think you got the last good woman. Everybody loves Lauren." He slaps his hand on the table. "So what can I do to help?"

Travis smiles. "Honestly?" Gabe nods. "Please tell me that you won't wear that maintenance uniform to the wedding. Buy a suit, dude. I'm begging you."

Gabe smacks the table, laughing.

Six

Maddie sets up the game Connect Four and waves for Amy to join her. "Would you like to play this with me?" Maddie sits at the end of the table, looking up at her. She picks up a red chip and slides it into a slot.

Amy agrees, sitting in the corner chair. "I'd love to! It's been years since I've played this." She picks up a black chip and taps it to her forehead, thinking of where to place it.

"You should know that I'm really good!" Maddie drops in another chip.

"I believe you!"

"I like your bracelet." It's a simple braided bracelet of turquoise, blue, and yellow.

Amy slides a chip into a slot. "Thanks! It's called a cord of three. See, it's got three heavy cords that are braided together because a cord of three can't be broken."

"It can't?"

Amy shakes her head. "Nope. A cord of

two can be flimsy but a cord of three is much stronger."

Maddie slides in another red chip. "I like the colors. It's pretty."

"Here," Amy says, loosening the bracelet from her wrist and sliding it off her hand. "You can have it. See, it slips on over your hand and then you tighten it by moving this bead up."

Maddie's mouth drops open. "This is so cool! I love it! But won't you miss it?"

Amy reaches for a black chip. "I got it at the flea market. The next time I'm there I'll pick up another one."

Maddie drops in another chip and grins. "Connect Four!"

Amy bugs her eyes out. "You *are* good at this!"

"Do you want to play again?"

"Sure!"

Maddie moves the lever so the chips will drop to the table and then moves the lever back in place. "Do you think Lauren will change?"

Amy looks at her. "What do you mean?"

Maddie studies where she should place her first chip. "After she gets married. Do you think she'll change? Because I don't want her to."

Amy shakes her head. "I think Lauren will

be exactly the person that you love right now."

"Mr. G. said that he changed. Said he was a bad husband."

Amy drops in a chip. "The guy that you wanted me to meet? He was a bad husband and you want me to meet him?!"

Maddie looks at her, rolling her eyes. "He *was* a bad husband but he would be a good husband *now.* He said he wasn't very nice to his wife. Do you think Lauren's husband will be nice to her?"

Amy looks over at Lauren, who's helping with the choir. "Lauren strikes me as a person who would be very careful and selective about who she lets into her life. Although I've never met him, I can assume that her fiancé is a good man."

Maddie drops in another chip, grinning at Amy. "Do you want to get married?"

Amy puts a hand on her hip with an exaggerated sigh. "Do you?"

"I'm too young!"

"So am I!"

"You're not young! You're old!"

Amy slaps her hand down on her thigh. "Miss Glory never told me that I was signing up for this!"

Maddie grins. "Well, you're not old but you're old enough to be married. I still think you should meet Mr. G."

"The guy who was the bad husband, right?"

"I think he should come to the fund-raiser and meet you. Don't you?"

Amy sighs. "I will be helping at the fund-raiser so if it makes you happy, then yes, tell him to come and I will be happy to say hello to him." She leans closer for emphasis. "I will say *hello* to him."

Maddie uses a hand to pat the air in front of her. "I get it. I get it. You'll say hello and that's it." She slides in another chip and points to the grid. "Connect four!"

"That's not fair! You keep distracting me!"

Maddie giggles and moves the lever again so all the chips will fall. "You're fun to play with."

"Only because you keep beating me!" Amy looks over at Maddie and smiles. "You said that a nurse named you." She's not sure how to continue with this train of thought but Maddie steps in for her.

"She did. The woman who had me was out of there." She raises her thumb and throws it over her shoulder as if hitchhiking.

Amy stops playing the game. "What do you mean?"

Maddie shrugs. "All I know is that she had me and then she left. My dad too."

Amy nods. "Their leaving had nothing to do with you."

"How do you know? I think once they found out I had CP they left." Maddie drops a chip into the grid.

Amy leans onto the table. "You can't tell that a baby has cerebral palsy when she's born."

Maddie looks at her. "That's what my foster mom said too."

"And she's right!" Amy says. "I worked with a woman with cerebral palsy and she was around your age when she was diagnosed. You can't look at a brand-new baby and diagnose CP. Your biological parents didn't leave you behind because of that."

"But how do you know?"

"Because no one could ever look at your face and walk away."

"I still wonder why they did."

"They were probably too young. Maybe her parents didn't even know that she was about to have you and she had you without their knowing. Maybe he had a drug problem and they thought that they were doing the best thing for you by leaving you in the care of someone healthy and strong." She desperately wants to believe this and hopes that Maddie believes it too. Maddie's face is blank, leaving Amy to wonder if she has said something she shouldn't have.

"They *did* do the best thing!" Maddie says, sliding another red chip into the grid. "I never would've come to my first foster home in Grandon, which means I never would have ended up with Linda. She took me to all my doctor appointments and helped me with my leg braces when I had them. She's a great foster mom." She thinks for a second and then says, "I never would have met my teachers or friends at school, or Mr. G., or Miss Glory, or you, or anybody here. Right?"

Amy smiles, nodding. "Right! And my life would be awfully dull without you in it." She drops a chip into the grid and realizes that she has just set Maddie up to win again and she groans, throwing her hands on top of her head.

"Thanks!" Maddie laughs, sliding her final red chip in to win.

Lauren and Stacy call for Maddie's group to come sing and Amy says, "Go on! I'll clean this up." As she's leaving, Maddie leans in to hug Amy's neck and Amy can feel her heart swell.

"She's awfully sweet, isn't she?"

Amy looks behind her at Gloria and nods. "She seems to have so much against her but . . ."

"But she's got everything going for her," Gloria says, finishing her sentence. "There's a lot to be said for childlike faith."

Amy begins to put the chips into the box and pulls the grid apart. "She said she's in a foster home. Is it a good home for her?"

Gloria hands her the lid to the box. "Her foster mom, Linda, is a lovely person. She's a nurse and has given excellent care to Maddie. She's an older woman who's been fostering for years. We need more foster parents like her."

"How have you done this for as long as you have?"

Gloria sits on the edge of the table. "Are you asking me how have I continued to believe that life for some of these kids can be changed, that somehow all their broken pieces can turn out for good?" Amy nods. "I believe because I've seen it happen in so many of their lives. I saw it happen in my own son's life. He ran away when he was a teenager, just two weeks before his father died, and was gone for years. All I had left was hope and faith. All I had was my prayers for him. I left my front porch light on every single day year after year, just praying that the light would lead him home, and it did. It seemed impossible that I'd ever see him again but I couldn't let my hope and faith die. I had to believe that my son would return. I have that same kind of hope and faith for these kids and I show that to them through the work that we all do here. And I pray for them every day."

"And that's enough?"

"It is enough because faith can move mountains." She laughs. "You learn a lot about mountain moving at my age!"

Miriam shouts for Gloria from across the big room and Gloria shakes her head, sighing. "I always thought the English were supposed to be demure. Miriam has shattered that image."

Amy puts the game away and turns to listen as the children practice "O Holy Night." When she was a child she did believe that faith could move mountains but that belief began to crumble as she grew into adulthood. There is a hollowed-out place in her heart that longs for a simple faith like that of Maddie and Gloria; a faith that sustains her when life pulls the rug out from beneath her. But the rug has been pulled out from under her one too many times, leaving her faith crippled at best. It wasn't her parents' fault. She looks back fondly at her home life with her two brothers and mom and dad. Her parents have always been supportive, and when her heart has been broken, her father's arms have been the first to surround her. It has been years since her heart was broken and she knows it's time to step out in faith, believing, like Gloria, that the broken pieces in her life can turn out for the good.

SEVEN

"Good-bye, Mr. G.!"

Gabe turns as he's folding the flag and walks toward Maddie, who's waiting for the van for Glory's Place. "Hey! You're first in line for the van today!"

"I decided to wait until I got to Glory's Place to go to the bathroom." He finishes folding the flag and puts it under his arm. She notices something on his arm and says, "I have a bracelet like that!"

He looks down at his corded bracelet of black, brown, and red on his arm and touches it. "We have the same great taste!"

"Miss Jenson gave this to me. She said that a cord of three can't be broken."

He nods, impressed. "That's right!"

"It looks like you and Miss Jenson already have things in common," she says, grinning and raising her eyebrows up and down.

He chuckles. "I think this is a pretty common bracelet."

"Where'd you get yours?"

He shrugs. "At an arts festival in California. I've had it for years. I don't know why I decided to put it on today."

"Miss Jenson got hers at the flea market."

"She probably paid less at the flea market. Those colors are really pretty on you."

She reaches out to touch his bracelet. "I really like yours."

"Then why don't you have it?" He begins to take off the bracelet.

"Really?"

He slides it over her hand. "Absolutely! Two of them will look awesome together. If I want another one I'll go to the flea market this time."

Maddie grins. "Maybe you'll see Miss Jenson there." She straightens her shoulders. "Wait! You have to come to the fund-raiser. She'll be helping out and she said that if you're there that she'd say hello." He begins to shake his head. "Please come! We are going to be singing and everything."

He sighs in resignation. "How can I say no to singing and everything?"

As the van pulls in to the school driveway, Maddie throws her arms around Gabe's waist. "It's Saturday morning, okay?"

He helps her into the van and watches as it pulls away. Before he was married, Gabe

71

always thought he wanted three or four children, but as alcohol gained its control, life became increasingly more about him. By the time he was married he had little interest in children. Life was a party and children would bring an end to that. His wife wanted kids but he always had the best of excuses: they needed more money, a better place to live, better health insurance, or more time together. The last excuse is laughable now as the more time they spent together, the more he tore them apart. He walks back into the school and through the empty halls to the maintenance office, placing the flag on its shelf. God saved him from destroying himself and this job has kept him busy, his thoughts and time occupied with others and not just himself.

He's tried dating a few times over the last six years but the women have never measured up to his ex-wife. She was kind and beautiful and would laugh at even his dumbest jokes. He dreads meeting Maddie's Miss Jenson but he will do it in order to see the joy on Maddie's face. Although he enjoys all of the children at school, there's something about Maddie that stays with him after he locks the doors each evening. He grabs his tool belt and bucket of tools and heads toward the gymnasium.

One of the risers was unable to be pulled out for the school assembly today and needs his attention.

Bent over his work, he wonders what he could do for Maddie and other kids like her. Although his dad wasn't perfect, he always showed Gabe the value of hard work and being a man of your word. He showed him how to be a man, and when Gabe's life fell off the rails, he always remembered his dad's words and example. What about the kids who don't know what that's like? He's heard rumblings of a mentoring program but knows little about it. Maybe there's room for someone like him to help? He jumps when he hears his name. "I'm sorry, Gabe," Mrs. Kurtz says. "I took a shortcut through the gym. I was trying to let you know I was behind you so that I didn't scare you but ended up doing that very thing."

"No worries. See you tomorrow, Mrs. Kurtz." For reasons he can't explain, and before there is any time to think of something else, he says, "Mrs. Kurtz?" Her hand is on the door as she turns to him. "I've been thinking . . ." She's looking at him, waiting, but he doesn't know how to put the words together. "I don't know."

She walks over to him and smiles. "What is it, Gabe?"

He turns the wrench over in his hands, looking down at it. "There are a lot of great kids here but . . ."

"Did one of mine do something? It's okay, you can let me know and I'll take care of it."

He shakes his head. "No. Nothing like that. I know it sounds strange but . . . I've heard about a mentoring program after school and was wondering if you know anything about it. I know there's lots of kids who could . . . I mean, I know I'm not the best example of —"

She cuts him off. "You would be a wonderful influence on so many of them! Mr. Parrish organizes that. I don't know much about it but I know that he tries to get some kids together with men once a week. The problem is he doesn't have enough men." She smiles. "He'll be so happy to know you're interested."

Mrs. Kurtz leaves the gym and he turns back to his work. He stands, thinking, wondering if he'd be any good at something like this. He turns the wrench over and over in his hands before setting it down on the riser and heading for the main office. "Is Mr. Parrish still in?" he asks Mrs. Kemper.

"He's in his office. Do you need him?"

Gabe rests his hands on top of the counter.

"I just wanted to ask him a quick question if he's around."

Mrs. Kemper shrugs. "You can head back there and see if he's available."

"Thanks," Gabe says, walking through the office to the hallway where the principal, school nurse, bookkeeper, and Vice Principal Parrish have their offices. Rick Parrish looks to be in his late forties and has been at Grandon Elementary for twenty years, serving the last eleven years as vice principal. Gabe sees that his office door is open and sticks his head inside. Mr. Parrish is working on his computer. "Mr. Parrish? Do you have a minute?"

"Sure, Gabe! What's up?"

Gabe sits in a chair opposite the desk, leaning forward on his knees. "I was just talking to Mrs. Kurtz and she said that you organize a mentoring program and I was wondering if you could tell me about it."

Mr. Parrish's face opens in surprise. "Absolutely! I try to pair a man from the community with a child from the school who currently lives in a home without a dad. We just get together once a week as a group and do things like bowling, go for pizza, or to a sporting event that's in season; sometimes we do a project. Ed came from the hardware store and instructed us on how to make a wooden airplane. Another time we made a simple boat together. Sometimes we'll just shoot baskets or play games. We discovered that it doesn't really matter what we do. The kids just like to get together." He props his elbows on top of his desk. "Could you help us?"

Gabe nods. "Yeah. I think so."

"Well, you've already gone through all the background checks so if you're interested you can join us tomorrow evening. We're meeting here at six for pizza and then someone's going to help us make a wreath for each child's front door."

"I'll be here."

Mr. Parrish leans back in his chair. "Just curious. What is it that brought you to me?"

Gabe shakes his head. "Maddie was telling me this week about her report on Florence Nightingale in Mrs. Kurtz's class. She said that if she dressed nice, she'd get extra points for her presentation, but she wasn't sure if what she wore was nice enough. I told her she looked perfect, and, I don't know why, but I've just been thinking of her and so many of these kids who don't . . ." He stops, thinking. "I know I'm not a dad but these kids need to hear that they're smart and awesome. Maybe I can help them believe that."

Gabe leaves the office unsure of what he's gotten himself into but there's no turning back now.

EIGHT

That evening, Travis and Lauren as well as Stacy and Miriam meet at Gloria's house for dinner because Lauren and Travis have asked them to help with the wedding plans. "First things first," Miriam says, setting the table with Gloria's dinner plates, the ones with the word *Thankful* — surrounded by autumn leaves — written across each one. "The date that you get married will often be determined by the place you select to get married." She sets the last plate down and moves aside so Stacy can follow with the napkins and silverware. "So," she says, moving to a cupboard to retrieve glasses. "Where do you want to get married?"

Lauren smiles, looking at Travis. "In the gazebo."

"I love it!" Gloria says, pulling a casserole from the oven. "Weddings in the gazebo are always so beautiful."

Miriam grabs a notebook off the counter

and sits at the table, taking notes. "Wonderful! And what day in the spring or summer are you looking at?"

"We were kind of thinking next month. On the twenty-first," Lauren says.

Miriam drops her pen and looks at them, dumbfounded. "In December? In the freezing cold? In the gazebo, where the wind comes whipping through there at eighty miles an hour?"

Lauren puts a napkin at each setting. "I didn't even think about it until we drove by there last night and I saw that the gazebo is gorgeous this year. That star on top is so beautiful and lights up the town square. As we drove by it I realized that the gazebo is what brought Travis and me together. If it hadn't been for the fund-raiser last year, we might never have met."

"Oh, you would have met him eventually," Miriam says. "The town isn't *that* big! Why don't you wait until it's warm? That way we can decorate with flowers like wisteria. Wisteria doesn't have a chance in the gazebo next month."

Lauren smiles at her. "We're not really looking for a lot of flowers or decorations, because the gazebo is already so beautiful."

Miriam's eyes widen. "And cold. Did I mention cold?"

"We are just looking for something simple," Travis says, sitting down at the table, facing Miriam. "We knew that if anyone could pull off a wedding this fast, it would be you."

Miriam nods. "Well, that's true enough." Gloria, Stacy, and Lauren glance at one another, smiling. "But I don't understand the hurry. Why December? I mean, the snow and ice and wind and . . ."

"Because all of you were there with me last year at the gazebo for the fund-raiser and the Christmas parade," Lauren says. "Gloria, don't you remember? You told me about Christmas miracles on one of the first days that I met you and one extraordinary thing after another happened to bring all of you into my life."

Gloria sets the casserole on the table. "Of course I remember, babe. If you want to get married in the gazebo, then by golly you are going to get married in the gazebo! Even if it means that all of us are out there in parkas or snowsuits. Right, Miriam?"

Miriam sighs. "Speaking of Christmas miracles, we should all start praying for one so that we don't get frostbite during the wedding vows. So the twenty-first is a Saturday? A Friday?"

"It's a Wednesday," Travis says. "The

gazebo is totally booked every weekend."

"A wedding on Wednesday?" Miriam says. "Who gets married on a Wednesday?"

"People in Paraguay get married on Wednesday all the time," Gloria says.

Miriam turns to her, her eyes simmering. "If you are going to lie, could you at least make it plausible. If you had said Boon Town, Georgia, or wherever it is you're from, that would have been believable, but you don't know anything about Paraguay!"

"I know they probably wouldn't welcome you there," Gloria says, whispering.

Stacy jumps in to change the subject, before filling the last glass with spiced tea. "Is Marshall eating with us?"

"Don't pour him anything yet," Gloria says. "He told me he might be late. They're doing Christmas inventory at the store and although they don't need him around for that, he likes to be there." Gloria married Marshall Wilson less than two years ago and they still consider themselves newlyweds, much to Miriam's chagrin. She places a bowl of green beans and another filled with coleslaw on the table. "Sit. Sit." They each take a seat as she opens her hands, reaching for Lauren's and for Miriam's, squeezing her fingers around them. "Lord, we're thankful for each other and for this food and for all the help you give us at Glory's Place. We're especially thankful for Lauren and Travis and the life they'll have together. Show us how to help them and keep our big noses out of where they don't belong." Miriam groans as the others snicker. "In Jesus' name I pray, Amen."

"God doesn't like irreverence, Gloria," Miriam says, scooping a hearty serving of casserole onto her plate.

"But he does like truth," Gloria says, plopping a scoop of casserole onto her plate and smiling.

"Let's get back to the wedding," Miriam says, ignoring her. "What about the rings or the wedding dress or reception hall? Do you have a bridal party selected or know what you would like them to wear?"

"We're getting together with the jeweler this week," Travis says.

Miriam writes something on the notepad. "Very good. Do you know what sort of dress you would like?"

Lauren takes a bite of the coleslaw and makes yummy noises in the back of her throat, pointing at her plate and giving a thumbs-up. Miriam puts her fork down and waits for her to respond. Lauren feels the urgency, wiping her mouth with a napkin. "I haven't thought too much about that."

Miriam scratches onto the notepad. "Then we must give that some thought right away. The good news is there are some lovely stores if we go into the city."

"Well, I don't really know if I need to go into the city. There are nice stores here."

"In a sweet, *Andy Griffith Show* kind of way, yes," Miriam says, not understanding. "But if you want upscale, we simply must leave Grandon."

"I don't want upscale," Lauren says. "I'm not even completely sure that I know what that means. I just want —"

Miriam lifts her hand to stop her. "Reception hall? Of course the nicest in the area would be at Laurel Glen. They have exquisite food and a wonderful space for dancing."

"We were kind of thinking we'd hold it at Glory's Place if that's okay. We'd like all the kids to come."

Gloria claps her hands together, trying to swallow the bite in her mouth. "That is a wonderful idea!"

"That is a horrible idea," Miriam says.

"Glory's Place has special meaning for them," Stacy says. "That's where Lauren met Travis to talk about the fund-raiser inside the gazebo. It's where she met you and Gloria, Dalton and Heddy, and where she helped me with the choir."

"Well, the theater that I worked in when I met my first husband had special meaning but I didn't want to serve coronation chicken there following my wedding ceremony!" She looks at their blank faces and presses her fingers to each side of her temples. "Have you thought about what you would like to serve?"

"We were thinking about chicken wings and potato salad," Travis says.

Miriam shakes her head as she shrugs, her arms open in front of her as if she's holding something huge. "Is this a wedding or a hootenanny? How about some mini quiches, along with cut vegetables and a nice pâté?"

"Miriam, I guarantee you that a room full of kids has never heard of quiche or pâté, but they do know chicken wings!" Gloria says.

Miriam leans back in her chair, defeated and resigned. "Will there be a cake?"

Lauren keeps her voice quiet. "We were kind of thinking of something like a long table filled with different kinds of candy." Gloria and Stacy look down at their plates as they stifle a laugh.

Miriam shakes her head. "No! No! No! It is a wedding. There simply must be cake. Surely children have heard of cake, right,

Gloria?"

"We're just trying to keep things simple and assure that we can afford the cost," Lauren says.

"Marshall and I want to buy the cake," Gloria says.

"No, Gloria," Travis says. "That's not the point. We —"

"We already talked about it and want to buy the cake. Or the candies. Whatever you want."

"They want cake," Miriam says.

Lauren begins to protest. "We don't need —"

"Yes you do," Miriam says. "You need a cake and this is Gloria and Marshall's gift. It would be rude to refuse."

"Okay," Lauren says.

Miriam sighs, scribbling on the pad. "After a plate full of chicken wings I refuse to choke down a handful of Gobstoppers."

"So everything is under way!" Stacy says. "Who knew it would be this easy?"

"Well, certainly not me!" Miriam says, flinging her notebook aside.

NINE

Amy closes the computer lid on her desk and slides it into her bag. Work as an insurance adjuster has kept her busy for four years, but each morning when she wakes, it feels more and more like a job. She enjoys the people in the office and the ones that she meets inside their homes or workplaces, but deep inside she wishes for something that seemed to have slipped from her many years ago. There's a monotony in her days that's making her feel used up and spent. More and more she finds herself anticipating being with the kids at Glory's Place. Nothing is the same there; the kids have brought a newness to her life that she wasn't aware she was desperate for. She was starving but didn't realize she was even hungry until the kids came into her life. "You're here!" Maddie says, making her way to Amy. Amy wraps her arms around Maddie, feeling the small, birdlike shoulders. "Guess what I get to do today?"

"Well, let me think," Amy says, walking to the lockers, but she's taking way too long to answer for Maddie.

"I get to go to Beside Me tonight."

Amy hangs up her things, looking at her. "Is that a movie?"

Maddie takes hold of her hand and leads her to the game area. "It's a thing at our school for kids who don't have dads. Mr. Parrish asked me today if I could come and he called my foster mom and everything to set it up."

Amy sits on a chair and waits for Maddie to find the game. "That sounds awesome!"

Maddie nods, dealing UNO cards to herself and Amy. "I'm nervous."

Amy picks up her cards, looking at them. "Why?"

"I'm always nervous when I meet new people."

Amy gasps. "Since when? You're like a social butterfly fluttering through this place. You make everybody who comes through those doors feel like part of the family!"

"It's different here," Maddie says, playing a draw-four card.

Amy growls, picking up four cards. She's already off to a rocky start. "You just be yourself and everybody there will love you."

"I don't think that always works. I'm myself in class but Jaron doesn't love me. He doesn't even like me. He doesn't like anybody."

"Well, those people are everywhere in life." Amy grins when Maddie lays a two down, winning the game. "I can't wait to hear all about what you get to do tonight."

"I already know! Mr. Parrish said we're going to make a wreath for the front door. I'll give it to Linda."

"You really like Linda, don't you?"

Maddie nods, passing out new cards. "She's really nice. Like a grandma."

"Would you like to be in Linda's home forever?"

"I really do like her. But I'd like a mom and dad and Linda as a grandma." She says it as if checking off items that are needed in the kitchen pantry: rice, beans, noodles, mom, dad, and grandma.

Questions whirl inside Amy's mind about how Maddie has gone seven years without being adopted, but she keeps those thoughts tucked away.

The rest of the afternoon is spent helping Caleb and Maddie with math, going over spelling words with Heather, reading with Aidan, Nicholas, Kaylee, and Brianna, shooting baskets with Logan, Alex, and

Ryan, and playing games with so many kids that she loses count. There are moments when she finds herself stopping and listening to the children as they practice their songs for the Christmas fund-raiser. She wonders if there's a sweeter sound than that of children singing "Away in a Manger" and tears fill her eyes as Maddie sings out with all her heart. When will her childhood innocence be lost? When will her wonder be replaced with cynicism? As she prepares to leave for home, Amy is tired but not weary, such a different feeling from a typical day.

"Amy!" She turns to see Gloria hurrying toward her. "Are you about to leave?" Amy nods. "I feel awful. The vice principal of the school called me this morning to let me know that Maddie is participating in something there tonight."

"She told me about it."

Gloria slaps her hand to her head. "I forgot all about it. I wrote it down. I even put a reminder on my crazy phone but I don't know how to operate that thing very well. Anyway! It starts at six, which is in five minutes and Maddie isn't there."

"Would you like me to drop her off?" Amy says, smiling.

"You really would be helping a crazy old lady out! I'm supposed to be meeting with a young mom who needs to enroll her children and I can't be in two places. Maddie's foster mom doesn't even get off work until seven and Lauren can't leave because she's the one who locks up and . . ."

Amy's moving toward Maddie as she says, "I'm happy to do it!"

"You are a lifesaver! I owe you one!"

Amy helps Maddie with her jacket and backpack and leads her to the car. "Now I'm really nervous," Maddie says, getting into the backseat.

"Just remember that all those men are there because they want to be. It's just like everybody at Glory's Place. We are all there because we want to be. Nobody twisted our arms or made us do it. We all chose to do it. We chose you," she says, smiling at Maddie.

Thankfully, the school is only five minutes away, and after she parks, Amy jumps out of the car to help Maddie with her things. The office is empty but they follow the noise to the art classroom just down the main hall. They are about to walk inside the room when Mr. Parrish exits it, nearly bumping into Amy. "There you are, Maddie! I was just coming to see if you had arrived."

Amy squeezes Maddie's shoulder. "Sorry she's a little late. There was some confusion getting her here but that won't happen again."

He takes Maddie's backpack from her. "Ready?" She nods, waving good-bye to Amy.

Amy lifts her hand in a small wave. "Have fun. And remember, I want to hear all about it on Monday!"

"I don't think I need to introduce you to your partner for tonight," Mr. Parrish says, leading Maddie inside the room. He points to the back of a man talking with two others.

"Mr. G.!?" Maddie shouts, surprised. Gabe turns and walks toward her, pulling her shoulders into his side. "I didn't know you were going to be here!"

"Well, I knew I was going to be here but I didn't know you were going to be here until a few minutes ago."

She smacks her palm to her forehead. "Miss Jenson just dropped me off! You could have met her."

"I can meet her when she picks you up."

Maddie shakes her head. "My foster mom is picking me up." She crosses her arms over her chest. "Guess what? I'm not even nervous anymore."

"Me neither!"

She looks up at him. "You mean you were

nervous?"

He nods, bugging his eyes out. "Yeah! Until I found out that you were going to be beside me. See what I did there? This is called Beside Me and I said I was nervous until I knew you were going to be *beside me* and —"

She holds up her hand. "I got it, Mr. G.!"

He laughs, patting her on the back. "I'm still a little nervous though." She looks up at him. "If you need somebody to work on the plumbing, I'm your guy. But I don't know anything about making a wreath. I'm glad you're here to help me." She smiles and he lifts his hand for a high five.

Sixteen kids are paired with sixteen men from the community. Many of them have just come from the office, now wearing tie-less shirts, others are wearing hoodies or jackets with the name of a heating and AC company, an auto repair, or a car wash embroidered on the front.

"I've never seen you in nice, real clothes," Maddie says, picking up a slice of pizza and putting it on her plate.

Gabe looks stricken. "Don't you like my blue maintenance uniform?"

She scrunches up her face. "Not really. I like that shirt better."

He looks down at the flannel shirt he's

owned for years. "I have a closet full of these."

"I like it. It smells nice. Like you just washed it." They sit at a table full of other men and children and Maddie giggles.

"What's so funny?" Gabe asks, biting into his pizza.

"I've never seen you eat. I've never seen Mr. Parrish eat either. It's weird!"

He grins, remembering something. "I saw my sophomore math teacher in the grocery store one day when I was with my mom. She said hello to me and I froze. She finally said, 'Yes, Gabriel, I go to the grocery store!' " He shrugs. "Who knew? Then she said, 'See you tomorrow,' and I said, 'And the day after that and the day after that.' I was so shocked to see her that I didn't know what to say. I had no idea why I said that! It was so stupid!"

She giggles with a mouth full of food. "It didn't make any sense."

He laughs. "No! It didn't."

"She called you Gabriel?"

"Yep! Adults do that sometimes for effect."

"Sometimes Linda calls me Madeleine for effect."

"Does it work?"

She thinks for a second. "Sometimes she

has to say it two or three times for effect before it works."

He leans toward her and says, "That's usually how things worked at my house too."

The entire room buzzes with the chittering of small voices clamoring for time well spent with this group of men who were strangers to them just two months earlier. Maryanne Shrupe, a mom of three who works at the local craft and hobby store, leads them through the wreath-making process. The entire room erupts in laughter as men who are used to working with wrenches, car tires, heavy equipment, or computers try to wrap fabric around circular Styrofoam.

"I'm sorry. I'm so sorry," Gabe says, fumbling with the fabric with his rough hands. He sees how much this tickles Maddie and keeps it up throughout the project. The other men have also found an easy way to get a laugh and Maryanne has all she can do to retain order. Once the fabric has been glued down, they work together to decorate with ribbon and craft autumn leaves. "You poof up the ribbon and I'll wire it down. I understand wire a lot more than ribbon," Gabe says. As a team they bunch up the ribbon, hold it in place, and then secure it with wire, all the way around the fabric.

"It's beautiful!" Maddie squeals.

"It's not done yet!" Maryanne says, walking behind her. "Now it's time to dress it up."

Gabe uses the hot glue gun and Maddie puts fake pumpkins, gourds, and autumn leaves into place as Maryanne instructs them. When it's finished, Maddie throws her hands on top of her head. "I can't believe it! It's awesome!"

Gabe holds the wreath out in front of him. "We made a wreath! I've never made a wreath in my life!"

"Can I give it to Linda? My foster mom?"

"You bet! That way she'll always have something that will remind her of you."

He didn't know why he said that. It came out of his mouth as if one day Maddie would not be in that home. But if not there, where? Maddie is too excited to pay attention to what he did or did not say and chatters brightly as he walks her down the hall and out the front doors. Linda gets out of the car when she sees them coming.

"We did this all by ourselves!" Maddie says. "It's for your front door."

Linda marvels at the wreath in her hands. Her hair is mostly gray and the lines around her eyes crease together as she smiles. "This just made my day. Thank you, Maddie!" She looks at Gabe. "And thank you. I know she loved doing this."

Gabe smiles and helps Maddie inside the car. "See you tomorrow, *Madeleine*!" He emphasizes her name, making her smile.

"And the day after that. And the day after that!" She begins to giggle, teasing him. "I have no idea why I said that!"

"I do," he whispers, as he watches them drive away.

TEN

It's a beautiful but unusually warm November afternoon for the Glory's Place Concert and Fund-raiser. The storefronts and buildings around the town square are dressed with twinkly lights and evergreen and a Salvation Army bell ringer stands in front of Wilson's Department Store, announcing the season of giving to shoppers and passersby. The star on top of the gazebo is beginning to cast a warm glow in the first shadows of dusk and Gabe tilts his head to look up at it through the truck windshield. Most of the parking spaces are already taken so he finds a spot a couple of blocks away, grabbing his jacket from the front seat in case he needs it. It's crowded around the gazebo but he cranes his neck, looking for Maddie. She spots him first and hurries down the steps of the gazebo to get to him.

"You came!" She's wearing a red sweatshirt with the words GLORY'S PLACE stretched across the front in white letters, along with a silver scarf and matching hat.

"You're as pretty as a Christmas present," he says, patting her on the back.

"Come on! We're about to start. Come meet Miss Jenson."

Gabe smiles, following her. He had already resolved when he got up this morning that he was going to make the best of this and do it for Maddie.

"Miss Jenson!" she says, tapping her shoulder. Amy turns at her voice and her smile fades. "This is Mr. G."

He is stunned. His face looks paralyzed as he whispers, "Amy."

Amy shakes her head. "No. Oh no!"

Gabe's heart pounds in such a way that he knows Maddie must hear it. He fumbles for something to say, feeling uncomfortable and terribly self-conscious, even embarrassed. "Amy. I didn't know."

"You know each other?" Maddie says, delighted.

"You said her last name was Jenson," Gabe says, his voice flat and lifeless.

"It is."

"It's Denison," he says, correcting her.

"I thought Miss Glory said it was Miss Jenson. They sound alike."

Gabe shakes his head. "Not even close."

Maddie looks up at him, oblivious to what she's done. "I need to go take my place. I'll see you both later, okay?"

Gabe's heart is beating loudly in his ears and his back is covered with sweat. He unzips his jacket to cool off. An awkward, clumsy silence stretches out as the singsong voices of children chatter around them. "She told me that *Miss Jenson* was single," Gabe says, unable to make eye contact with her.

"I am single, Gabe. You know how all that came about."

He glances at her. "I heard you were engaged so I assumed you were probably married by now."

Amy's hands are sweating but she can't let Gabe know how unnerved she is. "I don't know where you heard that. I'm not married."

If he could bolt from here he would but there's no place to run in the middle of all these kids and parents. "My mom heard it from your aunt and —"

"Your assumptions were wrong," Amy snaps. People shuffle around them to take their seats but Gabe and Amy continue to stand, uneasy with each other and unsure what to do next.

"Amy, I wouldn't have come if I'd known

it was you." He thinks for a moment and shakes his head. "Actually, I would've come because I'm here for Maddie." He looks at her and feels his throat tighten; he has so much to say, so much to make right. "I'm sorry this is awkward for you. I don't mean to . . ."

Amy shakes her head. "You don't need to apologize for this. Like you said, we're doing this for Maddie. I'd do anything for her."

He looks at her. "Yeah, me too."

Gabe follows behind as she walks to the rows of chairs; he realizes that she has changed her perfume and she's wearing glasses. Her hair is different too. It's longer now and a darker shade of brown, but she's still beautiful to him. He knew that if he ever saw her again, she would still be beautiful and she is. He finds a seat a couple of rows behind her, and as the children sing, he notices that Maddie keeps looking, searching for him, so he smiles and waves when her eyes meet his. The crowd surrounding the gazebo is large, there must be at least three hundred people sitting and standing nearby, but he's not aware of who's sitting around him or what's on the tables nearby for the silent auction; he's only aware of Amy. How could this have happened? How can she be a few rows away from him after all these years? When Lauren leads the children in "Joy to the World," tears fill his eyes at the words *Let every heart prepare Him room.* His heart was so full of himself years ago that there was no room for Amy, let alone God, but today his heart is different.

At the close of the concert, Gloria, Miriam, Dalton, and Heddy make their way into the gazebo to begin auctioning items for the fund-raiser. Gabe knows they're talking in the background but he can't hear them. All he can hear is the sound of blood rushing through his ears.

"Did you like it?"

He turns to see Maddie beside him and wraps his arm around her, hugging her. "I loved it!"

She grabs his hand, pulling him to Amy, who bends down to squeeze Maddie. "Even though I've heard you practice all of the songs," Amy says, "they sounded completely different inside the gazebo. It was just awesome!"

"Are you going to look at the auction stuff?" Maddie asks Gabe. "You might want to buy something!"

"Sure," he says, glancing over his shoulder at the tables. "I could use a basket filled with soap and candles."

"Miss DENI-SON," Maddie says, exaggerating the name to get it right, "can show you everything while I go back to the gazebo." She runs to be with her friends, leaving Gabe and Amy together.

"You don't really need to show me what's —"

"It's all right," Amy says coolly. "It won't take that long."

They walk to the tables lined with baskets filled with all sorts of goodies, generous donations from the community to help Glory's Place, and Gabe picks up a basket, examining the contents. "There is a gift card in there for a day of pampering at the spa, nail polish, hairbrushes, a new hair iron, and a gift card for a new cut and color with Randy at Hair Raising Experience," Amy says.

Gabe shakes his head. "If only the hair color had been with Leon, then I would have been all for it!" He notices Amy try to hold a smile away from him and picks up another basket. "How long have you been working at Glory's Place?"

She keeps her head down, pretending to study each basket. "I don't work there. I volunteer a few days a week after work. I started last week."

He feigns interest in a basket while watching her. "Do you still work at Redmond?"

"No. You're still working with your dad?"

"No. After you and I . . . I work at Grandon Elementary, actually. In the maintenance department." She nods. "If you don't work at Redmond, then where?"

"I work in insurance," she snaps.

"Insurance? I never knew that you —"

She stiffens, a fierce look crossing her face. "I think we can stop pretending to be interested in each other's lives. We're looking at this stuff for Maddie. That's it!"

He sets the basket down. "I'm not pretending. I want to know what you're doing. For six years I've wanted to know, Amy. I thought you moved away. I thought you were engaged."

"I did . . . and I was," she says, not wanting to look at him but holding his gaze. "I don't live in Grandon. I had to get out. How could I stay here and run into you? I was engaged. I'm not anymore."

"Look, Amy," he says, beginning to raise his hand to touch her arm but instead putting it at his side. "You don't have to tell me how I messed up because I know!" Her eyes are steely but he presses on. "I'm embarrassed to see you. Embarrassed by my behavior toward you. I destroyed us. I know that! And if I could go back, I would. I would go back and I'd change everything." He shakes his head, groping for the right words. "I think about you every day. Every day, Amy! I think about how I would apologize and hope that you would believe me. I think about the things that I said to you, how I treated you in the last six months of our marriage that were pure hell. And I think about . . ."

"How would you do it?" She looks at him. "You said that you thought about how you would apologize. How would you do it?"

After so many years of going through the words in his mind, when faced with her, he can't remember how he put the words together. "I would say that I know I was a bad husband. I was a bad son. A bad person. I was all about me all the time. Alcohol took that person to a whole other level and I let that person destroy us. That person nearly destroyed me. I'm sorry for all of it, Amy. I'm sorry for who I was and what I did, because you deserved the world. And you still do."

She glances away, clearing her throat. "Thank you, Gabe. Thank you for telling me that. And I forgive you. Actually, I forgave you three years ago because I couldn't let bitterness eat me up anymore."

"Do you think maybe sometime we could —"

"No," she says. "No."

"I was just thinking that we could get a cup of coffee. That's all."

She holds up her hand to stop him. "I understand, but no."

He nods. For years he had wanted to see her face-to-face and apologize and he has. He can't expect her to sit down and talk about old times because there's very little to look back on with any sort of joy or happiness.

"Are you buying anything, Mr. G.?" Maddie is standing with her foster mom, Linda, who is holding a fake floral arrangement.

"I won the bid," Linda says, lifting the arrangement higher. "It will look perfect in my living room."

Maddie looks at the table, still covered with baskets, and then back at Gabe. "Have you found one you like?"

He glances back to the table and notices one filled with Armor All, tire shine, window cleaner, car deodorizer, and a gift card to the express car wash and oil-change business down the road. "I think I'm getting this one."

"Whoa!" Maddie says. "That basket is one hundred dollars! Can you afford that?"

He laughs, picking up the basket. "I can afford it because the money is going to one of my favorite causes."

"I hope you have money left over," Maddie says.

"I have so much money left over that I was wondering if I could take you to Betty's Bakery for dinner after you're finished here?" He glances at his watch and up at Linda. "I can drop her off a little after seven."

"Yes!" Maddie says. "Can Miss Denison come too?"

"I can't," Amy says, jumping in.

"Why not?" Maddie says.

Amy can't think fast enough. "I have to go to —"

Maddie is impatient. "Where? Can you go there after we eat? I really want you to go. Please?"

"Gabe?" Gabe turns to see that Travis is staring at him in disbelief. "Hi, Amy," Travis says, trying to mask the surprise in his voice.

"How do you know Amy?" Lauren asks.

Travis looks at her. "How do *you*?"

Lauren laughs. "She volunteers at Glory's Place!"

Travis looks at Gabe. "I didn't know you guys were here together —"

"We're not," Gabe says. "Amy is the new

person there that Maddie wanted me to meet."

"Oh," Travis says. His eyes get bigger, realizing. "Oh! Wow. Okay." He lets out an uncomfortable laugh. "This is awkward," he says beneath his breath.

"How do you and Amy know each other?" Lauren asks again.

"She's Gabe's ex-wife."

"Ex-wife?!" Maddie yells.

ELEVEN

Betty's Bakery is crowded. By the time Gabe helped Travis, Dalton, and other men clean up all the tables and chairs at the gazebo, and cleared up the entire area, the crowd seemed to be of one mind: eat at Betty's Bakery. Gabe spots a small, two-top table in the back corner and leads Maddie there, pulling over an extra chair from a nearby table.

"I'm so glad you could come with us," Maddie says, as Amy sits across from Gabe. Maddie takes the third chair, positioned between them.

"Guilted into it is more like it," Amy says, trying to smile.

"Well, you did say that you wanted to hear all about my night at Beside Me."

Amy bobs her head. "Yes, but I assumed you would tell me Monday at Glory's Place."

"You assumed wrong," Maddie says, making her smile.

Travis was right: this is awkward, and every time Gabe and Amy make eye contact, they glance away to Maddie, or the sugar dispenser, or find great fascination in their silverware. But Gabe finds himself glancing at Amy again and again. Her eyes seem browner and her skin more radiant, her smile is more brilliant and her laugh is filled with an ease he's never heard. She is more beautiful than he remembers, and despite his best efforts, he can't will himself to stop looking.

"Gabe was my partner last night at Beside Me!"

Amy is surprised. "Really? You didn't expect that, did you?"

"I didn't expect it either," Gabe says. "But we had a great time. All the kids did."

"We made the best wreath ever and I gave it to Linda."

Amy leans back in her chair, smiling. "I bet she loves it!"

"It looks awesome on her door! Me and Gabe could make you one!"

Amy begins to shake her head. "Oh. No. That would be too much trouble."

"No it's not! Is it?" Maddie says, looking at Gabe.

"No. It's no trouble at all. As a matter of

fact, we're experts at it now and might very well star in our own DIY show on TV."

Maddie giggles. "What does *that* mean?"

"Do it yourself," Gabe says matter-of-factly. "Because that's what we do . . . We do it ourselves. And we do it amazingly!" Maddie laughs and high-fives him as Amy observes, wishing she was home.

They each order a different sandwich, and to make sure the conversation never lulls, Amy says, "I can't wait to see how much money you raised at the fund-raiser."

"I hope it's a million dollars!" Maddie says. She sips her lemonade and sets it down with a thud. "So! You were married!" Gabe and Amy nod, both hoping not to have to explain their marriage to a seven-year-old. "But now you're friends again," she says, smiling. Neither of them reply. "Right?"

Gabe looks at Amy. "I hope that we can be but sometimes adults can't make their way back to being friends the way that kids can."

This sounds absurd to Maddie. "Why not? Kids fight and then they make up. It's the same thing with you, except you're taller."

Gabe thinks for a moment and then says, "Maybe it's the height thing that's the issue."

Maddie looks at Amy. "Gabe told me that

he was a bad husband but I know that he makes a really good friend."

Amy forces a smile. "I'm sure he does."

"Do you remember why you were friends with him?" Maddie says, taking another sip of lemonade.

Amy twists the napkin in her hands, glancing away. "He made me laugh."

"He makes me laugh too!" She kind of bounces in her seat as she looks at Gabe. "Why were you friends with Miss Denison?"

"Because I thought she was the kindest person I ever met. I still think that about her." He glances at Amy and she catches his eye for a moment before looking at Maddie.

"So he made you laugh," Maddie says to Amy. "And you still think she's kind. And pretty, right?" Gabe clears his throat and Amy looks over her shoulder, hoping the waitress will arrive with the food. "Right?" she says, pressing further.

Gabe nods. "Yes. I think she's very pretty." Amy is so uneasy; she can't make eye contact with him.

"So maybe we can all go to a movie," Maddie says, shrugging, as if all is settled and happiness has been restored.

The food arrives and, thankfully, the conversation turns to Maddie. "You should

hear her presentation about Florence Nightingale," Gabe says, biting into his sandwich.
"She is very smart!"

"I know," Amy says. "She beats me at
every game we play."

"And she's friends with everybody!" Gabe
can see that Maddie is puffing up with pride
in front of him. "If Maddie sees that somebody needs a friend, she will be that friend."

"She became my friend right away," Amy
says. "Of course she got my name wrong
but I can forgive her for that."

"Denison sounds like Jenson," Maddie
says, her mouth full of food.

"Again . . . not even close," Gabe says,
making her howl with laughter. "Not even
in the same ballpark!" Maddie giggles, her
mouth gaping wide with food, and Amy
can't help but smile. Whatever heartache
and pain happened years ago between Gabe
and Amy appears to be temporarily forgotten. Forgiveness and mercy seem to hover
above this blue-and-white-checked tablecloth, entering each of them with, for the
moment, a sense of gladness.

"So what do you like to do when you're at
Linda's house?" Amy asks.

Maddie pops a potato chip in her mouth.
"I like to play with Teddy, her dog. And I
like to play video games, and read some

112

books, not all books, because I don't like books about boys or boogers and stuff." Gabe and Amy smile as they listen. "And I like to play games and go outside and ride my bike in the driveway. But I'd love to play the piano."

Gabe's eyes widen. "You could learn!"

Maddie shakes her head. "I could never play like this," she says, her hands racing over the tablecloth.

"If anybody could do this," Gabe says, his hands mimicking hers, "it's you!"

"I doubt it."

Gabe looks at her, banging his coffee cup on the table. "If you doubt that you can do that then you don't know the same Maddie that I do. The Maddie I know tries anything and never gives up. The Maddie I know races in the three-legged race on field day."

"And came in last," Maddie says.

"But she could have chosen to not race at all; however the Maddie I know said 'I want to be in the race'!" She smiles, raising her eyebrows when she looks at Amy. "The Maddie I know takes part in square-dance week in gym."

"It's awful," Maddie says to Amy. "People with CP should not square-dance."

"But the Maddie I know would rather dance than sit on the gym risers."

She begins to giggle. "I'm horrible at square dancing!"

"All of you are," Gabe says, deadpan. "The whole week is hideous to watch." Maddie and Amy laugh out loud together. "If I had a broom that could clean up the whole disaster, I would use it, but I just have to stand by and wait for the catastrophic mess to end."

"It's not *that* bad," Maddie squeals.

As much as Amy wants to remember Gabe as the wrecking ball that he was, she can't keep from wanting to believe that he has changed. There is a gentleness to him that she never knew. There's compassion and warmth for Maddie that he never showed for anyone when she was married to him. His laugh is easier and his tone is light; when they were married his words were edged with hardness. She doesn't want to be here, sitting in this small space seeing this side of him. It's easier to think of him the way he was.

"Here come part of the triumphant fundraising team!" Gloria says. Amy looks over her shoulder and is relieved to see Gloria and Miriam, Stacy, and her son, Ben, walking toward them. Their presence will take some of the strain away.

"Miss Glory!" Maddie says, leaning over

to hug her.

"I'm Gloria," she says to Gabe. "And this is Miriam."

"Gabe Rodriguez," he says, shaking her hand. "It was awesome! The kids were amazing," he says, looking at Maddie.

"Each year I think that it was our best fund-raiser ever and we could never top it but then the very next year the kids prove me wrong! And of course I keep getting the very best volunteers," she says, winking at Amy.

"And of course the staff who has been there from day one is an integral part of each success," Miriam says, a bit offended. "Dalton and Heddy and . . ." She stops for effect.

"And you, Miriam," Gloria says, sighing. "Whatever would I do without you?"

Miriam smiles, satisfied. "How do you know Maddie?" she asks Gabe.

"I work at the school and, as you probably know, Maddie is a superstar there."

"And you know Amy! How wonderful," Gloria says.

"He loves her," Ben says, making his mom's mouth drop open.

"Ben!" Stacy says.

"He does. He loves her. Don't you?"

Gabe clears his throat and coughs, accidentally spilling his coffee when he covers his mouth. He scurries to use his napkin to sop it up.

"They used to be married," Maddie says, moving away from the brown stream headed her way. Amy wonders if her face has fallen, just as her heart has.

"Oh!" Miriam says. "Isn't that something? That's wonderful to . . . I mean, it's so nice to see . . . just something, isn't it?" She looks at Gloria for help.

"Well, you both have a tremendous friend in Maddie," Gloria says, bailing Miriam out.

"I've seen you in my line at Clauson's," Ben says to Gabe. "I'm Ben. Remember me? I bag your groceries."

"Of course! You put the notes in each customer's bag," Gabe says, recognizing him. "You rock those notes, Ben!"

Ben smiles. "You don't buy a lot and you look different today than when you're buying groceries. You look happy. That's why you love her."

"Ben!" Stacy whispers, loudly enough so everyone can hear.

"I need to get going," Amy says, uncomfortable and scooting her chair back with a loud shriek across the floor.

"Yes!" Miriam says. "We all should go."

Gloria glares at her. "We just got here,

Miriam," she says, hissing at her. "Stop talking, okay?" Gabe and Maddie push their chairs out, standing. "We'll see you on Monday, all right babe?" Gloria says, giving Maddie a squeeze. "Thank you again and again, Amy, for all your help this morning."

"Nice meeting all of you," Gabe says, putting his hand on Maddie's shoulder and guiding her toward the door.

"That was painful," Miriam says, watching them leave.

"Only because you made it that way," Gloria says, sitting down in an empty chair.

"I'm pretty sure Ben helped usher in the pain," Stacy says, looking at him, smiling.

Ben looks sheepish and confused. "I just said the truth!"

Miriam sits across from Gloria. "Amy looked miserable." She watches the door close behind them. "What are you going to do about it?"

Gloria opens her mouth and raises her arms in a shrug. "What am I going to do about it? Nothing! My biggest question in life is what to do about you." Miriam rolls her eyes as Gloria and Stacy laugh.

Amy's car is two blocks away but it feels like it's taking them days to get there. She just wants this to be over. The star on the gazebo seems to shimmer in the night air and Amy wishes some of that light would enter her, lifting the darkness from her shoulders. When they reach her car, she unlocks it and gives Maddie a quick hug. "I'm so proud of you and the other kids! It was an awesome day!" She looks at Gabe and tries to smile. "Bye, Gabe."

Gabe lifts his hand in a clumsy wave and smiles as she gets behind the wheel. Maddie slips her hand into his and they watch as Amy backs up and leaves. *But not for good,* he says to himself, squeezing Maddie's hand.

TWELVE

For the last several years, Sunday has been Amy's favorite day of the week. Always a morning person, she gets up to attend the early service at church. It wasn't until after her divorce that she discovered the hope found in community. Faith and church had been a part of her childhood but once she went to college, she all but abandoned it. When her life was spiraling downward, she discovered that something was missing, something much bigger than the absence of a husband, and she returned to the faith of her childhood. For so many years she had formed her identity from what she did, or as Gabe's wife, but when they split up she felt like her identity was marred by the divorce. It was only when she began to read through the Bible that she came to know the God of all comfort and eventually returned to church. It was a Christmas Eve service, two years after her divorce, and as soon as a small ensemble began to sing "Silent Night," her eyes filled with tears. When the minister said, "Jesus was born for the one whose life is falling apart. Christmas is for the lonely and forgotten and for the one who is crippled in spirit," the tears raced down her cheeks. She became part of this band of believers and learned about forgiveness and hope in the darkest places.

After the morning service she declines the offer to join friends for their usual Sunday breakfast and heads back to her house, a small one she rented and eventually purchased in Cortland, the next town over from Grandon. To keep herself occupied, she pulls weeds from around the house for an hour or so, before sweeping out the garage and tidying the bathroom, but her thoughts are loud, nagging and frustrating her, making her feel disheartened. She eats a small lunch before grabbing her keys and heading out the door for the movie theater.

Showtimes are listed at the side of the ticket booth and she stands and reads over the movie choices. There's a special screening of a new animated movie, *Arthur Christmas,* before its release date, and Amy thinks it's just the thing she needs to lift her from this funk. The theater quickly fills with children and their parents. The notification

120

of this special screening must have gone to every elementary school in the area, but Amy doesn't mind. She enjoys the sound of their laughter. At the close of the movie, she sits and reads through the credits before standing to exit. "Miss Denison!" Maddie yells, walking down the stairs toward her. "What are you doing here?"

"I just came to the movies and saw that this was playing and thought it'd be great and it was! What did you think?"

"I loved it!"

"Where's Linda?" Amy asks, looking behind her.

"I'm here with Mr. G. He's up there," she says, pointing a few rows behind them. Gabe is standing with his hands in his pockets, watching them. He waves, keeping his distance so Amy can escape, but Maddie waves for him to come down. "I didn't know that grown-ups would go to a kids' movie by themselves."

Amy laughs. "Of course they do!"

Gabe smiles, approaching them. "So you still read through all the movie credits."

"And apparently you do too," Amy says.

"We're going to the park," Maddie says. "Can you come? Mr. G. says this might be the last nice day we have before it turns cold."

Amy smiles. "So Mr. G.'s a meteorologist now?"

Maddie scrunches her eyebrows together. "I'm not sure exactly what that is but yeah, he's the best." Gabe grins, sticking his hands back into his pockets. "I'll show you where I like to play dragon and castle. Okay?"

"I'm sorry. I can't."

Maddie's face clouds over. "Why not? It's Sunday. You don't have to work, do you?"

Amy shakes her head. "No, but I need to get —"

"Where?" Maddie asks, pressing her again and looking at her with enormous brown eyes. "Where do you need to be right away?"

Amy sighs. "Sure," she says. "I'll go for a few minutes."

Amy follows Gabe the few miles to the park and pulls in beside his truck. Maddie leads them to the playground area, spread out with swings, monkey bars, towers with swirly slides and swinging bridges, a sandbox, climbing poles, and more. "The castle and the dragon are over here," Maddie says, waving them on.

Gabe and Amy watch as she steps up to the swinging bridge, which leads to the tower. "Should we let her be doing this?" Amy says, concerned that Maddie's leg will make her unsteady on much of this equipment.

"She does it at school," he says, watching her. "Not much slows her down."

"How did you wind up at that movie?" Amy asks, keeping her eyes on Maddie.

He turns his head to look at her. "They announced it at school and sold special tickets. I talked about it with Linda a couple of days ago. Why?"

"Because it seems strange that people who live in Grandon would go to a movie in Cortland."

Gabe glances over at her. "So you obviously live here in Cortland now?" She doesn't respond. "If you're thinking that somehow I knew that and I came here just hoping to run into you somewhere in Cortland, that's not what happened. I bought these tickets on Friday, *before* I even knew you were in Maddie's life. Maybe you're the one who heard about the special screening and thought we would be there."

She snaps her head around, looking at him. "I did not!"

Gabe begins to smile. "Maybe you volunteered at Glory's Place because in the back of your mind you thought you'd run into me in Grandon."

"That's ridiculous! I drive straight to

Glory's Place and then I leave. Trust me, I did not want to run into you . . . accidentally or otherwise."

He chuckles. "You're the one who brought it up."

"This is where the dragon lives," Maddie says, waving to them from a window in the tower.

"If you need help slaying him then let me know," Gabe says. "I've slain plenty of dragons in my time."

"I can do it," Maddie says, making sounds as if she is struggling with the fire-breathing creature.

Amy watches Maddie play. "Have you?"

Gabe moves to a nearby bench, sitting down. "Have I what?"

She sits next to him. "Slain plenty of dragons."

"I have. All of them. All the ones that tried to destroy me, anyway."

She looks out, watching as Maddie makes dramatic moves inside the tower, defeating the beast within. "How'd you do it?"

He leans forward on his knees. "AA. I watched a man who worked for my dad clean himself up and I thought if he could do it, I could too."

She nods. "How many years?"

"I started a few months after we divorced.

I'm five and a half years sober."

"This is how I throw him down," Maddie says, pretending to toss something out the tower window.

"Ouch!" Gabe says. "That's it for him. Watch out! Look behind you!" Maddie turns and wields an imaginary sword. "My natural instinct was to explode at anything or anyone. After we split, for the first time in my life, I realized that I was capable of anything and that scared me to death. Now when chaos strikes, I don't explode because I know what I'm capable of. Problems aren't world-ending anymore."

Amy makes a noise at the back of her throat. "There's definitely been some sort of shift in you. That's for sure."

He watches Maddie and nods. "Yeah, a good humbling will do that."

"How is it that you're so good with kids now?"

"I think I was always good with them but I wasn't around them."

"And you didn't want them."

He looks at her. "I didn't know what I was missing. But I really love being around them. I even take college classes so I can be with them."

She studies him, surprised. "What are you studying?"

"Elementary education. I'm one of the old guys in class. Thankfully, a lot of classes can be taken online." Amy nods, letting it sink in. "I know. I never seemed like the college type." He thinks for a moment before saying, "You kept the bracelet."

She doesn't answer but watches Maddie play. "How do you know that?" she says finally.

"Maddie showed me the bracelet that *Miss Jenson gave her.* I didn't think anything about it until yesterday when I looked down at the bracelet on Maddie's arm and realized it's the same one I got you on our honeymoon. She said *Miss Jenson* got it at a flea market."

She shakes her head. "I never wear it but for some reason I put it on that day. When she said she liked it, well, I didn't see any reason for keeping it."

"But you did keep it."

"And so did you," she snaps.

He laughs, raising his hands in surrender. "I know! I kept it because it reminded me of what I did wrong. We were never a cord of three because I never wanted anything to do with God. We were a cord of two, and then just a single strand." They sit together in the quiet. Gabe rubs his hands together, thinking, keeping his eyes on the ground.

"Maddie asked yesterday if we could be friends again." He looks up at her. "Could we?"

Amy's heart begins to pound beneath her ribs and she sighs. "I know you've changed, Gabe. I see it with Maddie. I feel it just sitting here next to you. You're centered now. You're peaceful."

He waits for more. "And that would make me a good friend, right?"

"For other people. Not for me. It's all too strange."

He leans back on the bench. "I've always been strange so that shouldn't surprise you. And Maddie said I was a very good friend."

"She also said that you were a good meteorologist so I wouldn't put too much stock in what a seven-year-old says." Gabe smiles, watching Maddie. "I'm glad Maddie knows you. You seem good for her but you wouldn't be good for me. I know too much. Too much water under the bridge." She looks at him and can tell by the look on his face that she's been unusually harsh.

He is speechless and stands, walking to help Maddie down the stairs. "And that's how you slay a dragon!" he says, high-fiving her.

"Can we swing before we leave?" Maddie asks, looking at them.

"I need to get going," Amy says, hugging her good-bye. "See you on Monday."

Maddie doesn't notice that Gabe is silent as she leads him to the swings.

THIRTEEN

Miriam pulls a wedding dress from the rack at Grandon Dress and Formal Wear and holds it in front of her. "What do you think of this one?" Lauren touches the dress but is quiet. "Just because this is my gift to you doesn't mean I'm picking it out," Miriam says. "This is your dress! So, what do you think?" Lauren shakes her head. "Too Laura Ingalls? I agree." She reaches for another one, lifting it off the rack. "Well?"

"I don't know . . ." Lauren looks at Gloria. "What do you think?"

"I think you need to choose a dress that you love," Gloria says warmly.

"But Miriam, you're . . ."

Gloria holds up her hand. "This is your wedding and this is Miriam's gift to you. She's not the one wearing this dress. Right, Miriam?"

"Absolutely! You simply must choose the

dress that you love," Miriam says, meaning it.

Lauren walks down the racks of dresses, moving each one until she finds a simple white satin dress with capped short sleeves. "I like this one."

Miriam reaches for it. "But where's the train?"

"I don't want a train."

"You don't want a —" She stops when Gloria digs her finger into her arm. "Do you want a veil?" she asks, hopeful.

Lauren smirks. "Not really. I'm sorry, Miriam."

Gloria laughs. "You don't need to apologize to her! This is your wedding! Isn't that right, Miriam?"

"Of course it is! But I think you'll find that they have trains that can easily attach to the dress that would elongate and beautify it in a dramatic yet elegant —"

"Miriam!"

Miriam nods. "But elegance isn't for everyone."

"Always classy, Miriam," Gloria whispers.

"I like this one too," Lauren says, lifting one in breezy polyester. "And this one."

Gloria and Miriam wait outside the dressing room and ooh and aah as Lauren models each dress. Lauren never thought something like this would happen to her. It was just one year ago that she sat waiting in a restaurant booth for her mom to show up, after years of being gone from her life. She never showed. Lauren thought that was the summation of her life and she failed to return to Glory's Place for days on end, but then Travis showed up. He waited outside the grocery store where she worked as a cashier and wouldn't let her walk away from Gloria, Miriam, Stacy, and all the kids at Glory's Place. He encouraged her to show up again and she did, and now she's staring at herself in wedding dresses.

"I asked Dalton to give me away," Lauren says, looking at the back of one dress in the mirrors.

"When did you do that?" Gloria asks, reaching for a pack of M&M's in her purse.

"Just yesterday. I drove over to their house and he and Heddy had just finished lunch and were about to eat some cake."

"Was it her hummingbird cake?" Gloria asks, popping an M&M in her mouth. "She makes the best hummingbird cake."

"It was red velvet."

"Mmm," Gloria says with enthusiasm. "That one is the best." She notices Miriam staring at her and pops another M&M into her mouth. "Go ahead."

131

"So Heddy gave me a piece of cake and a cup of coffee and I asked him."

"How did you ask him?" Gloria says, helping her unzip the dress.

"I said, 'Dalton, you're the closest person to a father that I've ever had and I would love it if you would walk me down the aisle at my wedding.' " Dalton and Heddy had an open-door policy with Lauren. She ate with them a couple of times every month, played games with them and their grandchildren, helped get their flower beds in shape in the spring and fall, and stood nearby as Dalton changed the oil in her car. They hugged her and Travis each time they arrived and hugged them good-bye when they left.

"And did he cry?" Gloria asks. "Dalton always cries."

"He did. Heddy did too."

Gloria claps her hands together. "Oh, I love it! They think of you as another granddaughter."

"Their white/Hispanic granddaughter," Lauren says, laughing.

"Families are made up of all colors," Miriam says.

Gloria looks at her. "That was lovely, Miriam."

"Oh, shut up," Miriam says, sighing.

Seven dresses later, Lauren decides on the first one she found, the one in white satin with the short, capped sleeves. Her size is unavailable but they are told it will only take five or six days to receive. Lauren hugs both Miriam and Gloria for their help and vows to remember this day forever.

FOURTEEN

Amy races inside Glory's Place, aggravated that she could not get out of the office earlier. "I'm so sorry I'm late," she says when she sees Gloria.

"Don't worry about it, babe," she says, taking a math book from Lukas. "I used to be in the workforce too." She glances over the work in the book and looks up, spotting Stacy. "Stacy? Would you take Lukas back with your group? He needs some extra help with multiplication. Run on back with them," she says, handing the book back to him.

"Um, Gloria," Amy begins. "I think I need to explain."

"Explain what?"

"About Saturday at Betty's Bakery. I never told anybody that I'd been married before."

Gloria smiles. "You didn't have to."

"Well, it was awkward and . . ."

"Only because Miriam made it that way,"

Gloria says. "That's one of her gifts that just keeps on giving. Of course Ben didn't help much either, did he?" She squeezes Amy's arm, laughing, and begins to walk toward the tutoring room.

"I don't know why Ben said that," Amy says. Gloria turns to look at her. "Gabe doesn't love me anymore."

"I just can't believe that," Gloria says. Amy looks surprised. "It seems that once someone meets you they'd love you forever." She smiles and begins to step away.

"Um, Gloria! I was wondering if I might be able to chat with you at some point," Amy says.

"Sure. Let's go to the office and I'll have Heddy oversee tutoring today." Gloria closes the office door behind them and sits in a chair next to Amy.

"I had a thought a few months ago and I thought it would go away but it didn't."

Gloria nods. "One of those hanging-on thoughts."

"At first I thought it was a bit crazy but as time went on, it made sense, and I told you that I had taken the courses to be a foster parent." Gloria nods. "That's where you come in."

"I'm happy to help!"

Amy shifts in the chair. "From my very

first day here I looked at all these kids and thought that I could easily bring any one of them into my home and take care of them. That's how I felt about them. Right from the start." Gloria nods in understanding. "I know that several of the kids here are in foster care and if there's a time down the road where you know that one of them needs a new foster home . . . well, I would love to open my home."

"You would be wonderful! Have you met Patricia Anderson with the Department of Family Services yet?" Amy shakes her head. "She's a longtime friend and the social worker that we most often work with; she can answer all of your questions. She'd know if all of your paperwork is in place or if you're missing anything. If you're ready, I can call her."

Amy nods. "I think so."

"Patricia has helped with a lot of the kids who have come through here over the years." She looks at her. "I'm glad you're following the nudge."

"Is that what it is?"

Gloria nods. "It's what I call it. God nudges us throughout our lives but I wonder how many actually act on it."

Amy walks out into the big room, looking across it, and wonders how many nudges she has ignored throughout her life. Maddie, Eva, and Brianna grab her for a game of Sorry! and she looks at their faces, fully believing she's not supposed to miss this nudge.

Gabe reaches for the milk and closes the refrigerator, before pouring a couple of his favorite cereals into a bowl. After the divorce, he lived with his parents for a few months before securing this apartment. It is sparse; he's never needed much: a couch, a TV, a small table with a couple of chairs, a bed, a nightstand, and a chest of drawers. His life has been routine for the last several years: get up, eat some cereal, go to work, attend AA, meet with his sponsor, and develop his relationship with God. He is the first to say that God saved him from himself. He accomplished more in his first thirty days of sobriety than he ever had before in his life and is still amazed at what he can do sober. For years his natural survival skill was to turn to alcohol alone; he thought every day had to be lived in the highs. He had to create a new natural order to his life and in so doing he has discovered that life is pretty darn good in the middle.

This morning he seems to be following his normal routine, and it feels that way, but his thoughts are far from normal. If anyone had asked him two weeks ago if he would ever see his ex-wife again, he would've said no. If that same person had asked if his ex-wife would ever sit next to him on a bench and laugh, he would have said no. If that person would then ask if Gabe would ever find himself having feelings for his ex-wife, he would have answered a resounding no, but today something has changed. He spent a fitful night thinking about her, about her laugh, about her penetrating eyes when she's challenging him on something, the little creases that appear on each side of her mouth when she smiles, and the ease and kindness she displays when interacting with Maddie. As much as he wanted to drive the thoughts away so he could rest, there she was again and again. When she first saw him at the gazebo, with the initial recognition, sorrow appeared in her eyes, and it made him cringe, knowing that he was responsible for putting it there. But he noticed, first at Betty's, and then on the park bench, that the look in her eyes changed; it became a look of confusion. The look of grief and sorrow is too much to bear, but he can handle bewilderment, because it possibly means that she's trying to figure out what has happened to him, that maybe she's recognizing he's no longer the same.

During the lunch hour for the fourth-graders, Gabe and Lenny, one of his co-workers in the maintenance department, continue to work on returning heat to Mrs. Navarro's room. The heat and A/C system has been on its last breath for the last couple of years, which means Gabe and his coworkers are kept busy throughout the school. As Lenny leaves the room for extra tools, Gabe pulls out his phone, looking at it. The same thought that nagged him throughout the night has spilled over into the morning, but he's afraid to follow through. He slips the phone back into his pocket and tries to return to his work, but the phone feels heavy in his pocket and he pulls it out, tapping the map app and typing in *Glory's Place.* He wants to call and leave a message for Amy, or does he? He wants to make things better, but will calling her only make matters worse? When he hears Lenny's voice just outside the door, he slips the phone back into his pocket.

Fresh apple pie, cakes that are rising in the oven, chocolate scones on the counter, and percolating coffee fill Betty's Bakery with delicious smells as Amy enters the shop.

Gabe waves at her from a bench and stands when she approaches the front counter.

"Funny to see you here," he says, shoving his hands in his pockets to keep them from flying away.

"I'm picking up some pastries for a meeting that Gloria is having this afternoon." She looks inside the display case, hoping he'll go back to his seat.

"I just got out of class. I'm waiting for Travis and am a few minutes early. We meet here sometimes before he goes to help Lauren clean up at Glory's Place."

"Ah," she says, pointing to a variety of pastries for the woman behind the counter. "Gloria said there's also a pie that she ordered ahead of time." The woman nods and disappears behind the wall.

"So how were the kids today?"

"They were great," Amy says. "I could ask you the same thing about all the kids in school."

"I don't deal with them as much as the teachers do, but when I do see them, they're great."

A long and miserable silence stretches out between them and Amy sighs, looking down into the display case. "If I'm going to be bumping into you when I come to Grandon, how long is it going to take before anything between us gets past this uncomfortable hump?"

He smiles, nodding. "I don't really know how you want me to talk to you because you said that I wasn't good for —"

She cuts him off, remembering her harsh words. "Just talk to me like you talk to Travis."

He laughs. "I don't think so. Travis and I still act like idiots together."

She attempts to make their conversation sound relaxed. "I'm glad he's marrying Lauren. She's great. She absolutely loves those kids at Glory's Place."

"She is great. They were on-again, off-again for a while last year, and I wondered if they would make it but, man, Travis loves her and he chased her down, proving it to her."

"Sometimes a girl just needs proof, I guess." She looks at him a moment longer than she intended and glances at her watch, wondering out loud what has happened to the woman helping her.

"That color blue is very nice on you." She's wearing a blue turtleneck with blue jeans and looks amazing.

"Thanks. I've had this for years."

"Same with this shirt," Gabe says, tugging on the flannel collar. "But Maddie likes it."

"When did you become a flannel man?"

He glances down at the shirt. "I'm not really sure. One day after we split up I looked at my clothes and realized . . ."

"You needed to get rid of them and start new," she says, indicating the turtleneck.

"Well, I like your new look," Gabe says.

"Thanks. You're definitely a flannel guy now."

"And your hair and glasses are great. You started new with everything."

"I needed to." She smiles when she sees the woman return with the pie and boxed pastries and Gabe offers to help her out. "I got it. Thanks," she says, leaving him at the counter.

On his drive home, Gabe can't remember everything that they talked about, but he remembers her. Her eyes are now a mixture of puzzlement and something else; something that made his heart slip an inch or two beneath his ribs. It's too much to think about or imagine, but Gabe drives home smiling anyway.

FIFTEEN

Lauren waits at the front counter as the sales associate at Grandon Dress and Formal Wear goes to the storeroom to retrieve her wedding dress. The wait becomes lengthy, and assuming the woman has gotten caught on a call that she answered in the storeroom, Lauren decides to peruse the dresses on the racks. She notices a young woman around her age or older on the other side of the store who seems to be shopping with her mother. On closer look, Lauren realizes they are the same two women who were on the ground watching Travis as he put the star on top of the gazebo. They are whispering as they hold up a dress, checking out the price, before returning each one to the rack. A couple of minutes later, Lauren pretends not to notice as the would-be bride becomes visibly upset, her voice rising, and tears filling her eyes.

"There's nothing here that's affordable," the younger woman says, keeping her voice low. "Let's look somewhere else."

"Let's keep looking here," the older woman says, trying to calm her. "We'll find something."

"Mom. It doesn't matter. I don't need a dress."

Her mother puts her hands on her daughter's shoulders, forcing her to look at her. "You've dreamed of this day since you were a young girl. You've always wanted a wedding dress and your father would want you to have one."

Lauren studies pearls lining the sleeve of one dress but can see the young woman shake her head. "You don't have . . ." Lauren can't make out what she's saying as the sales associate is talking over the racks of dresses to Lauren as she reenters the store.

"I am so sorry," she says. "It's not in yet." She moves to the computer, clicking the keys.

"I was told it would be in this morning," Lauren says.

"Yes, you're right. It should have been, but for some reason . . ." She pecks away at the keys and nods, seeing the answer on the screen. "It's on back order. Hmm."

Lauren waits for her to clarify what *hmm*

means. "So . . . when will it be in?" she asks, concerned.

Lines crease between the woman's brows. "It shouldn't take more than three or four days," she says, looking at Lauren over her glasses. "We can call when it arrives."

Lauren decides not to tell Miriam; there's no reason to get her up in arms over a few days' delay and Miriam hasn't rebounded since Lauren told her that Stacy, her maid of honor, could wear whatever dress she preferred.

"No, no, no!" Miriam said, stomping her foot inside the big room at Glory's Place. "A maid of honor should exhibit class and elegance in what she wears, and I've seen Stacy at black-tie events. She's a solid, salt-of-the-earth gal and her wardrobe reflects that fine stock."

"I'm right here, Miriam," Stacy said.

"Oh, no offense, dear. I'm merely saying that a wedding requires something more than off-the-rack at Wilson's Department Store."

"Incredible. In one breath she's managed to offend not one, but two people," Gloria said. Miriam turned to her, annoyed. "My husband owns Wilson's, you know!"

"And so you know that there isn't anything upscale about it," Miriam said, as surely as the sky is blue and the grass is green.

Despite the dress not arriving on time, as far as Lauren is concerned, the wedding plans are nearly perfect.

Maddie wasn't at school yesterday and Gabe hasn't seen her this morning, so he assumes she's sick. This time of year always brings with it one or two viruses and the flu. As much he wants to, he refrains from texting or calling Amy, to touch base and see how her day is going. He wants to be that person in her life again but realizes it's probably impossible. However, she no longer looks at him with hate or bitterness and for that he's grateful. After their divorce it's actually more than he could have hoped for. He reminds himself to stay cool, keep his head on his shoulders, and his mouth shut, so he doesn't ruin any possibility of friendship.

As he walks by Mrs. Kurtz's classroom at lunchtime, he sees Maddie sitting alone at her desk, eating lunch. Mrs. Kurtz is at her desk, holding a sandwich in one hand and leafing through a stack of papers with the other. He knocks on the door before opening it. "Hello, Gabe," Mrs. Kurtz says.

"Hi. I noticed that Maddie wasn't in school yesterday and when I saw her sitting in here at her desk, I thought that maybe she isn't feeling well again today."

Maddie looks at her lunch, and Mrs. Kurtz is careful as she speaks. "She's physically fine but sometimes people can make you feel less than fine, right, Maddie?" Maddie nods, playing with the carrots on her napkin. Mrs. Kurtz smiles at Gabe, knowing that he understands.

"When I saw her I was wondering if she could help me get some tools from the maintenance office. I'm working in Mr. Glade's room, across the hall, and it would take me a few trips by myself to get all the tools but —"

"Absolutely!" Mrs. Kurtz says, smiling. "Maddie, do you think you could help Mr. G. for a moment?" Maddie shakes her head.

"It'd only take a few minutes," Gabe says. Maddie keeps her eyes on her carrots. Gabe glances at Mrs. Kurtz and she lifts her shoulders in a shrug. "Okay, I'll see you later, Maddie." He waits for a moment but she doesn't respond and he knows that something is wrong.

At the end of the school day, Gabe lowers the flag and folds it, noticing that the van for Glory's Place has already left. He missed saying good-bye to Maddie but sees her in the school lobby as he walks through the doors. "Hi, Mr. G.," she says sheepishly.

"Maddie! You missed the van."

She nods. "I know. I told the driver that I was sick and now the lady in the office is trying to call Linda at work."

"I'm sorry you don't feel well."

She shakes her head. "I lied. I'm not sick."

He kneels down in front of her. "What's going on? Why did you tell the driver that if you're not really sick?"

She looks at him. "Because I felt bad about not helping you today and wanted you to drive me to Glory's Place."

He smiles. "You don't need to feel bad about not helping me. I was just trying to get you out of the classroom to see how you were doing." He stands, extending his hand. "Well, let's go to the office and let everybody know that they don't need to call Linda at work to come get you. I'll be your chariot today."

Thankfully, Mrs. Kemper hasn't been able to contact Linda yet, so with the proper authorization filled out and signed, Gabe and Maddie leave the school together. They walk down the sidewalk stretching in front of the school and Gabe puts his hand on her shoulder. He's never realized how small and fragile she really is. "Rough couple of days, huh?" She nods. "Was it something another student did?" She nods, and they turn the corner to the parking lot. "Was it one student or more than one?" She holds up one finger. "Did the student do something or say something?"

"Said something," she says, staring at the pavement as they walk.

"Was it a student in your class?" She shakes her head. "Not your class. Can you tell me what the student said?"

"I don't want to."

"That's probably for the best because I planned on roughing them up."

She looks up at him, shaking her head. "You can't do that. You're a grown-up."

He smiles. "Kidding."

"Mrs. Kurtz talked to him but it probably didn't do any good."

Gabe opens the back door and takes her backpack, setting it on the backseat. He helps her inside and walks around the truck and slides in behind the wheel, starting the engine. She's quiet on the drive and as Gabe approaches Glory's Place he says, "You're sure you don't want to tell me what he said?" She shakes her head as he pulls to the front of the building, getting out and opening the back door.

"You know what?" he says. "It doesn't

149

matter what he said." She looks up at him, her eyes lacking their normal flashes of light. "It doesn't. No matter what he said, it doesn't define who you are." He kneels down in front of her. "You are smart, awesome, and a beautiful little girl with an amazing smile and this world is a better place with you in it." Her expression appears to question what he's said. "It's true. Just think about this world without you in it. Think about what that would mean for Mrs. Kurtz's classroom, or for Linda's home, or for Glory's Place, or for me as I work at the school every day. The world wouldn't be the same." Tears fill her eyes and her mouth stretches to a straight, thin line. She crumples into him and he pats her back. "It doesn't matter what he said, Maddie. Words hurt but it doesn't mean they're true."

She pulls away from him. "We were talking about Christmas and saying what we wanted. I said I wanted a pretty ring and he said that nobody would ever give a ring to somebody as ugly and weird as me. He said fancy gifts like jewelry are for normal people." Her lip begins to quiver. "I know everybody thinks that I'm weird. Sometimes I see people look at how I walk and I know what they think." She begins to cry. "They think I'm ugly."

He puts his hand on her arm, squeezing it. "Do you know what people think when they see you?" She doesn't answer. "Do you know what they think?" She shakes her head. "They think, What an awesome, beautiful little girl she is. What a great personality! She's so smart! What a beautiful name! They notice you. And nobody in the history of the world would ever think that you're ugly."

"I haven't been around for the history of the world."

"It doesn't matter!" Gabe says, detecting the beginning of a smile. "If you were over six thousand years old, no one in those six thousand years would ever have thought you were ugly. Yes, several of them would have thought you were weird, but we're all weird. My last name's Rodriguez and I don't like rice and beans! I'm half Hispanic! What Hispanic person doesn't like rice and beans? That's weird."

"I don't like olives."

"That *is* weird! I love olives." He cocks his head. "You missed a day of school because you felt so bad about what that kid said?"

She nods. "I told Linda I didn't feel good and stayed home."

"The next time that bully says something to you, just show up. Just showing up drives bullies crazy." He stands and begins to walk her to the door.

"Mr. G.?" she says.

"Yeah."

"I think just showing up drives the bad things away too."

He looks at her. "What do you mean?"

"Everything bad that that kid said was stuck on me. It was stuck in my brain. But then you showed up." She gives him a quick hug before slinging open the door to Glory's Place.

Sixteen

Wilson's Department Store shimmers and sparkles with all things Christmas: from the wintry scenes displayed in the storefront windows, to the giant ornaments hanging from the ceiling, to Santa's workshop located in the children's department. Gloria's husband, Marshall Wilson, and his team of employees work for months leading up to Christmas, planning and dreaming of how the store will look. Several years ago, Marshall created "Christmas Delights," a hot chocolate, spiced cider, and homemade cookies station where a customer could buy a drink and a cookie for a quarter each. Kids would always eat and drink for free. From the moment customers enter the front door, Marshall wants them to feel at home, especially at Christmastime. "A lot of folks aren't able to bake cookies or decorate their homes at Christmas, so I want them to feel the warmth and wonder of Christmas when they walk through those front doors," he has said to his employees year after year.

Lauren and Travis open the front doors and Travis inhales. "That smells like gingerbread," he says, raising his eyebrows in a grin. "Let's go see."

Lauren tugs on his arm. "No! Let's look for what you'll wear for the wedding first and then you can go buy a cookie." She shakes her head, sighing. "I sound like a mom talking to a four-year-old!"

"Listen, when I was a kid it rocked my world when Mr. Wilson set up that cookie and hot chocolate station! It rocked the world of every kid in Grandon. Kids got everything for free and adults could get a cup of hot chocolate and a cookie for twenty-five cents! And the price has never gone up. You go to Betty's and you're paying over four dollars for the exact same thing!"

She folds her arms, tilting her head when she looks at him. "I thought you loved Betty's?"

"This has nothing to do with my love for Betty's. This is all about keeping a childhood tradition alive."

Lauren groans. "Oh, good grief. Let's go get your cup of coffee and your cookie because you're good for nothing until you do."

He begins to lead her to the back of the first floor, where the Christmas Delights station is located. "Actually, it's a cup of hot chocolate. That's my childhood tradition. Not coffee."

"Whatever," she says playfully, holding his hand. They stand in line behind several parents with children. "Can I point out that everyone waiting in line is a child?"

He looks at her, dumbfounded. "When do you think childhood traditions begin? At twenty-four?"

As they wait, Lauren looks around the store, admiring the decorations and Christmas displays. Her eye catches a young woman in the dress department who looks familiar. She notices another woman with her and recognizes them as the mother and daughter who had helped put the star on the gazebo and who were at Grandon Dress and Formal Wear a few days ago. They are methodically pulling dresses from the racks and checking each price tag, before hanging them each back up. "I'll be right back," she says to Travis.

"Don't you want a cookie and hot chocolate?" His eyes are huge and eager and make her laugh.

"Okay, okay. But I want a cup of coffee with the cookie."

"Is this going to be your tradition? Cookie and coffee?"

She throws her hands in the air in mock exasperation. "Yes! I declare on this date that a cookie and coffee will be my official Wilson's Department Store Christmas Delights tradition."

"That's all I needed to hear," he says, turning to wait in line again.

Lauren walks up two stairs into the dress department, walking close to the young woman and her mom, and holds up a dress at arm's length in front of her, pretending to be interested in it. "There are other dresses downstairs, Mom. Let's go look there."

"They aren't going to be as nice as these," the mom says.

The young woman looks stressed but relieved, as if a long-awaited answer has come to her. "They won't be as nice as these but they couldn't be more perfect for what I need. As a matter of fact, I don't even need it. I could wear these blue jeans and this shirt and get married and still be completely happy."

Lauren can see the beginning of tears in the mother's eyes and turns her back to look at another dress, so they don't think she's listening. "But you need a beautiful dress for your wedding."

"Mom." The young woman's voice is firmer now. "Jared and I could go today to the courthouse and get married, and as long as you and Kristy and his family were there, it would be a perfect day for us. It's got nothing to do with a dress." Her mom opens her mouth to speak but the young woman will have none of it. "I know that Dad wanted me to have a beautiful dress but he never anticipated getting sick and neither of you knew what that would cost the two of you. You keep saying that Dad wanted me to have a beautiful dress and I will. And it will come from downstairs at Wilson's. Not from upstairs at Wilson's." She wraps her arm around her mom and leads her to the stairs. "We've always been downstairs-at-Wilson's kind of people anyway."

Her mom laughs. "That would never fit on a business card."

"Well, we've never been business-card people either." The mom rears her head back and laughs as they walk down the stairs.

Travis finds Lauren and hands her a cookie. "Just as I thought . . . gingerbread!" He takes a bite of his cookie and notices her face. "What's up?"

She shrugs. "Have you ever had a moment where you are just instantly sad? I mean, just like that," she says, snapping her fingers.

"I guess. Why?"

"I just heard a conversation that should have been really sad but somehow it wasn't."

"So it wasn't really sad but you were instantly sad listening to it?"

She smiles. "I know. It doesn't make any sense."

"How do you feel right now? I mean, standing here eating your first Christmas Delights cookie at Wilson's? Are you instantly angry? Instantly annoyed? Instantly miserable or depressed?"

She laughs. "I'm instantly delighted eating this Christmas Delight cookie!"

"Yes!" he shouts, handing her the cup of coffee. "Our first Christmas tradition together." He kisses her and she grins. Growing up, she never had traditions. Not one. But all that changes today.

SEVENTEEN

At five o'clock, Gabe opens the door to Glory's Place. Linda called earlier in the day to let the staff know that Gabe would be picking Maddie up today. Several children and Maddie are playing a game when Gloria informs her that Gabe is taking her home, and she jumps up from her place, grabbing her backpack and jacket.

Amy is helping two children sound out words at the reading circle and glances up to see Gabe waiting. She wonders if he's here to talk to her but notices that he's not craning his neck, as if looking for her. He's just standing there with his hands in his pockets. He never catches her eye but perks up when he sees Maddie walking over to him, and Amy watches as they leave together.

Maddie finds the perfect booth for them inside Betty's Bakery, and she slides into one opposite the pastry displays. "I still can't believe you picked me up for dinner today," she says, beaming.

"I just assumed that you ate dinner and since I eat dinner too, I thought why not eat it together? I told Linda that I would have you home by the time she gets home from work, and that we would bring her dinner tonight." He looks over the menu. "What do you think we should get her?"

"She loves casseroles. We eat a lot of casseroles," she says, kind of chewing on the words, which makes Gabe laugh.

"So I take it you won't be ordering any casserole?"

She shakes her head with her eyes wide, studying the menu. "No, I will not! I will be ordering this hamburger with fries and lemonade." She points to it, smiling.

The waitress walks to their table, bringing two waters, and takes Maddie's order first. "And I will have the same thing because I love hamburgers, but no lemonade with mine," Gabe says, handing the menu to her before she walks away.

Maddie slaps her hand down on the table. "We have a lot in common! We both liked the movie. We both like the park. We both love hamburgers. We both like Grandon Elementary School and Mrs. Kurtz. We both like Lauren and Travis and Miss Glory and Miriam and Linda and Dalton and Heddy and Amy." She thinks for a moment. "We like all the same people!" She slaps the table. "I almost forgot! All the kids are invited to Lauren and Travis's wedding. Are you?"

"Am I? I'm actually *in* the wedding!"

"You are? How?"

He laughs. "How? Travis is my cousin. He asked me to be his best man and I said yes."

She shakes her head, looking at him. "How did I not know that you were his cousin?" Her face looks vacant as she ponders this. "I've never really thought about it before but I don't have any cousins. That's weird."

"Plenty of people don't have cousins."

"How's that possible?"

He leans both arms on the table. "Because if you're an only child and you marry an only child, that means you don't have a brother or sister who has any children, and the man that you marry doesn't have a brother or sister, which means no children on either side. Or . . . you could have a brother or sister but they don't have any kids. Maybe your husband has a brother or sister but neither one of them has any kids either. Without any kids, you don't have any cousins. So it's not that weird."

She furrows her brow, trying to follow what he just said. "Okay. But I wish I had cousins."

"Travis and Lauren would definitely call themselves your cousins."

She points her finger at him. "But they're grown-ups and those aren't fun cousins. And anyway, how can they do that if they're not my family?"

He raises his arms in exasperation. "Do I have to explain everything?" he says, teasing her. "Families come in all shapes and sizes and colors. You know Stacy at Glory's Place?" She nods. "I don't know her, except for meeting her and Ben at Betty's Bakery after the fund-raiser, which, as you know, was way, way, way awkward!" She giggles listening to him. "But anyway! Lauren thinks of Stacy as an older sister and she thinks of Stacy's kids as a younger brother and sister. When Lauren moved here last year, she became part of their family."

"She told me that she didn't have a mom and dad either."

Gabe nods. "They were out there in the world somewhere, but they didn't take care of Lauren. She lived with a lot of families but she finally felt like she was *part* of a family with Stacy and her husband and kids.

And Miss Glory and all the others are extended family for her. Just like they are for you."

Maddie smiles. "I wish you were my family too."

"I'd like being part of your family because you make me laugh and you're so smart about stuff that I don't know anything about!" She grins at him but there's an underlying sadness in her face.

"Have you ever wanted to be a dad?"

He feels self-conscious and looks over his shoulder for the food, but knows it's too soon for it to arrive, forcing him to answer. "When Amy and I were married, I didn't want to be a dad."

"Why not?"

"Well, first of all, I was very selfish. And, I didn't think I would be any good with kids."

"But you are good with kids," she says, reaching for the lemonade the waitress has brought.

He lifts his shoulders in a shrug, nodding. "I like kids. I think they're awesome."

"So maybe one day you'll have your own."

"Maybe." He cocks his head, looking at her. "And maybe someday you'll have *your* own. Someday you'll look at a guy and think he's pretty cute and you'll want to marry him."

She recoils, her eyes opening in horror at the thought of it. "Yuck!"

"You say *yuck* now but one day, you never know, you might meet a boy and fall in love. Or, you might remain single and have a full, awesome life."

She raises her hand to stop him from talking. "I'm going single all the way." Gabe laughs out loud as the food arrives. "Is your life full and awesome?" He spreads mayonnaise on the top bun, looking at her. "You're single. Is your life full and awesome?"

He presses the bun back down onto his hamburger. "I heard you the first time. I'm just wondering when you became a talk show host."

She bites into her burger. "What's a talk show host?"

"It's a person on TV who gets all up in people's business, asking them questions."

"Do they get paid?"

He nods, chewing. "Yes! Way too much money."

"I'm in!"

He pounds the table, laughing. "You didn't answer my question."

"You are relentless. Yes. I think my life is awesome. But it could be fuller. How's that for an answer, Dr. Maddie?"

"It's good. One day you'll have to work

on the fuller part."

He stares at her. "Hmm. That's deep. Too bad I can't take you seriously with that blob of ketchup on your chin."

She reaches for her napkin and swipes at it. He knows what would make his life full, but he doesn't dare think about it.

EIGHTEEN

Patricia Anderson straightens the papers in front of her and puts them into a manila folder before handing them to Amy across her kitchen table. "I'll send these to you electronically as well, but these will be your hard copies. Do you have any questions?"

Amy sucks in air, making a sound of astonishment. "So everything's done?"

Patricia nods, completing her thought. "All of your paperwork is in order. Your training is done. Your home is lovely. The names that you provided gave you raving recommendations, as did Gloria and, as far as I'm concerned, if Gloria recommends someone as a foster parent, then I listen."

Amy sighs. "Suddenly, I'm nervous."

Patricia smiles, soft lines crinkling at the corners of her eyes. She's been a social worker for longer than she hasn't. It has been her life and her passion. "The nerves will go away. Trust me."

"You've met with other nervous potential foster parents?"

Patricia laughs. "I was one of those nervous potential foster parents! My husband Mark and I had lost our son." She doesn't allow Amy time to respond and says, "The grief took me . . ." She stops, trying to find a sentence to cobble together but can't, shaking her head. "It nearly destroyed me. It was destroying my marriage and we were nearly done but, thankfully, there were two little girls in different circumstances who needed parents, and God knew that we needed them."

"How old were they?"

Patricia smiles, pulling out her phone to show a picture. "Five and two. Emily's ten now and Mia is seven, but I was a wreck those first few nights with Emily."

Amy is careful how she phrases this next question. "Was there ever any difference in your love for —"

Patricia answers before Amy finishes. "At first, yes, because I was their social worker. I loved each of them as one of 'my kids,' " she says, making air quotes with her fingers. "I love all the kids that I help. I'm very protective. They're 'my kids.' But once they were in my home, something changed. They were no longer 'my kids,' they were *MY* kids.

Not all foster parents feel that way, because they know that they are fostering a child until he or she can be returned to the home of his or her own parent or parents. But that wasn't the situation for either of our girls. There wasn't a home to return to for either of them, and once Emily and Mia were in our home, I couldn't think of them going anywhere else because they were mine. They were ours." She shifts in her chair and raps her fingers on the table. "Are you looking to simply foster a child that will be reunited with the biological parent, or are you thinking of something lasting?"

Amy scratches her head, shaking it as she does. "When I started all this I thought of it as being something temporary but over the last couple of weeks I've been feeling . . ." She searches for the words. "I've been feeling that I'm ready to be a mom. I was ready several years ago but then the rug got pulled out from under me and I put all those thoughts on the back burner."

"But now the flames are burning higher and the water's about to boil over."

Amy laughs. "Exactly! I just don't know if I'm really ready."

"No parent is ever really ready but I've met a lot of parents who aren't as ready as you. Any child would feel safe and blessed to be in this home with you."

Amy pushes a crumb onto the floor, swiping her hand back and forth over the table-top in front of her. "I know there are kids at Glory's Place in foster care and if one of them ever needs a home I'd like to help."

Patricia stands, gathering her coat and purse from the back of the chair. "If a child becomes available, you'll be one of the first to know."

Amy walks her to the front door, opening it. "Thank you so much, Patricia. You've made this feel very easy for me."

"I'll be in touch."

Amy waves as Patricia gets into her car; she seems to feel her heart pressing against her ribs. She closes the front door and surveys her living room. Before long, there will be a child sharing this space with her. She moves down the hall to the spare bedroom and stands inside the doorway, looking inside. The small antique desk her parents gave her sits on the opposite wall; a vase of dried flowers and a Tiffany-style banker's lamp are positioned just so on the top. The lines of the maple chest of drawers and bed are clean and simple, as are the white comforter and pillows. Everything is neat, tidy, and orderly, much like the life Amy has created for herself in the last six years. She has managed to put together an existence without the intrusion of heartache and kept any sort of untidiness outside her door. She knows that once she opens her home to a child, her heart will be invaded once again and life will be messy, sometimes very messy. She walks into the room, pondering the thought.

NINETEEN

Grandon Dress and Formal called Lauren that afternoon and told her her dress had arrived. When Amy heard the news she offered to complete Lauren's shift that evening so that she could get to the shop before it closed. "I can get it tomorrow," Lauren said.

Amy put her hand on her hip. "Why would you do that? You know that you're dying with excitement to see it, so go!"

"But it's so late for you to stay."

Amy waved her hand in the air as she walked away. "I'm not listening to you anymore. I'm staying."

The store closes at six so Lauren leaves Glory's Place at five thirty. It's already dark outside; this season feels so long with darkness creeping in so early but she doesn't mind it today. The streetlamps are wrapped in evergreen and a banner stretches across the street, announcing the annual Christmas parade. She drives around the square and looks for the star above the gazebo — grateful that someone decided to buy a star so Travis could place it there for everyone to see — but it's not lit up. She's grown accustomed to seeing the light each time she drives around the square and thinks of how naked the gazebo looks tonight without the dazzle of the star. A parking space is available in front of Betty's Bakery and she pulls in, walking the block to the dress shop.

The bell jingles, announcing her arrival inside the store, and the same salesperson who had helped her days earlier smiles amid the dresses. "You're Lauren, right?"

"Someone called me today and said my dress is in."

"It's right here," the woman says, walking behind the counter. It's not hanging in a bag or packaged neatly inside a box, as Lauren had expected, but is displayed in full view, taking her breath away. "We always like for our brides to see the dress before we cover it up. Isn't it beautiful?"

Lauren nods. "It's actually more beautiful than I remembered." The saleswoman lifts it off the rack and hands it to Lauren. "Wow! I can't believe this is mine."

The woman smiles as she takes it back from her and gently places it inside a dress bag with the Grandon Dress and Formal logo on the front. "You'll be a beautiful bride." She walks around the counter, handing the dress to Lauren. "If it needs altering in any way, you just call us so we can schedule an appointment with the seamstress. Congratulations!"

Lauren leaves the store, beaming. Her steps are hurried as she walks down the sidewalk, the cold air makes her lungs catch. She can't wait to show Stacy and Gloria and Miriam. She's never been a girly girl, and never thought she would be excited about wearing a dress, but the weight of this dress over her arm, and what it means to her, nearly makes her giddy, and she's far from a giddy person! As she approaches her car, she looks over at the gazebo; the star on top that wasn't lit when she went inside the dress shop is now spreading fingers of light across the square. Her eye catches the young woman who was standing there the day the star was put into place; the one she's since seen at the dress shop and then at Wilson's. Lauren crosses the street and approaches her. Even though her knit cap is pulled tightly over her ears, the woman's cheeks are flushed from being in the cold. The woman notices Lauren and slips her hands into her pockets, pulling out gloves.

"Did you get it to light up again?" Lauren asks, pointing to the star.

The woman nods. "I shook the cord on the side of the gazebo. May be a little short in it somewhere." She's looking up at the star and the glow from it illuminates her face. "I'll let someone at the parks department know."

Lauren shifts the dress to the other arm. "I saw you here that day when you were helping to put it up."

The woman turns to look at her. "Not helping. Just watching. It's beautiful, isn't it?"

Lauren smiles. "It is. I love it!"

"It was my dad's idea. He thought of it in October and was really excited about it but then he was diagnosed with cancer and . . ." She looks up at the star again. "He died eleven days later. My mom and sister and I just had to put this up for him." She turns to look at Lauren. "No matter the expense, you know? He loved Christmas! He loved it so much that I wanted to get married at Christmas." She turns her face to the star, shaking her head.

Lauren peers up at it. "It's a beautiful tribute." She pauses, looking at the woman. "I'm so sorry that you lost your dad."

Tears swim in her eyes. "Me too. I'm

twenty-six years old but I don't feel old enough to lose a parent." She notices the dress bag over Lauren's arm and uses that as a means to change the subject. "Special occasion coming up?"

Lauren nods, choking back emotion. "My wedding. My fiancé, Travis, was actually the one who put the star up there," she says, pointing.

"Really? That was your fiancé? He was so nice. Funny too. He kept saying 'If I start to fall, run over here and catch me.' It was kind of an emotional day, for my mom especially, and he was just very kind to us. You're very lucky to be marrying someone like him."

"I agree," Lauren says, feeling tears begin to form.

"My fiancé is also a kind and funny guy. Guess we're two of the lucky ones. I'm Mandy, by the way."

"Lauren."

Mandy lifts her hand to wave. "Nice to meet you, and again, congratulations! I hope you have a great wedding." She turns to walk to her car.

"You too." Lauren turns and feels the wind against her face. She heads toward her car but stops, glancing back at Mandy. "Mandy!" she yells. Mandy turns to look at her. Lauren pauses as her heart pounds in her ears. She lifts the dress off her arm. "I . . ." She steps closer. "You and I look about the same size." Mandy's smile fades. "I would really like you to have this dress for your wedding."

"Wha . . . ? No!"

"Please don't say no. The gift for your dad on top of this gazebo has made Grandon shine. You've honored him in such a beautiful way. I mean, look at that! It's a bright star in a night sky! How many towns have something that beautiful? I believe that you would also honor your dad if you were to wear a beautiful dress on your wedding."

Mandy shakes her head. "I can't. I have a dress."

"But is it the one your dad would want you to have? He wanted you to have one, right?" Lauren can see Mandy's eyes glistening.

"This . . . I can't. It's yours and . . ."

"My friend Gloria tells me to hold things loosely but people close. I never had a tight hold on this dress. My hold is on Travis and Gloria and Dalton and Heddy and Stacy and the kids at Glory's Place, and Miriam, whom I'm going to have to explain all of this to, but I love her anyway." She begins to laugh and Mandy laughs out loud with her. She steps to Mandy. "Please take it."

Mandy covers her mouth; she is speechless. Lauren places the dress in her arms and hugs her. "I hope you have a beautiful wedding and a wonderful life together."

Mandy is overwhelmed as she hugs her back, tears rolling down her face. "Thank you doesn't sound like enough."

"I think the same thing when I see that star."

TWENTY

Amy drives past Betty's Bakery as she heads for home, but something catches her eye and makes her drive around the town square again, passing Betty's for a second time. There it is. Gabe's truck. She starts to drive away but something in her makes her slowly drive that loop around the square for a third time, and she pulls up in front of the restaurant, holding tight to the steering wheel. She remains here for several minutes, staring at the restaurant door as people come and go, battling with herself over what she's doing here. She rests her forehead on the steering wheel before turning off the engine. When she enters Betty's, she inhales a combination of smells — savory soups, pot roast, and mulled cider — and realizes how hungry she is; it's after seven thirty and she has normally eaten something by now. Gabe catches her eye from a booth and he waves, standing up. She takes off the hood of her jacket and walks to him, shoving her gloves inside the pockets. "So weird seeing you here again," he says.

She shrugs off the coincidence. "Just picking up something for Gloria again. Are you eating?"

"I was supposed to be meeting Travis but Lauren called him and said something came up that she wanted to tell him and Gloria about."

She nods. "I'm sure it was about her dress. I worked late for her so that she could go pick it up."

Gabe glances down at the table. "You're welcome to join me if you haven't eaten."

Amy purses her lips, thinking, as her head bobs up and down. "I'm really hungry and that sounds . . ."

She doesn't finish and Gabe says, "I haven't ordered yet so . . ."

They sit facing each other in the booth and Amy picks up the menu, looking it over. "Hard to believe that the wedding day is so close."

"Right. A little less than a month away."

She sets the menu down. "They don't seem nervous. That's good."

"Were you nervous?"

She looks at him. "I wasn't. I was ready because I was marrying the man I wanted to live with for the rest of my life." His mouth turns up in a sad smile. "I didn't mean for that to make you sad. I just remember that day so clearly because I wasn't nervous. It's not a sad memory for me. I'm sorry."

He shakes his head. "No. You don't need to apologize. That day isn't a sad memory for me either, but something inside me knew I wasn't the man that you deserved. Even then, I knew what I needed to do to be a man, but I didn't do those things. I thought that marrying this amazing woman would somehow make everything right with my world."

She leans on the table. "I'm really glad that everything seems right with your world now, Gabe."

He chuckles, running his fingers through his hair. "It took God awhile but, thankfully, He's persistent. I knew that if I wanted to live I needed to get sober."

"And you did."

"With a lot of help, yeah."

"And you have a job that you seem to like."

He smiles. "I do."

"And before you know it you'll be teaching inside a classroom. Will you stay at Grandon?"

He picks up the napkin and begins to fold it over and over on the table. "I hope there's a spot for me when I graduate. I really want to teach there."

"I didn't ask before . . . when will you graduate?"

"I have two semesters left."

She shakes her head. "I had no idea."

He shrugs. "There hasn't been a lot of time to . . . catch up."

They give their orders to the waitress and Amy sips her club soda. "I saw you drop Maddie off the other day. She hugged you and . . ." She turns her head to look out over the tables. "She trusts you, Gabe. She's crazy about you."

He shrugs. "I seem to be more charming to little girls."

"That's not true. Big girls find you charming too."

She holds his gaze and his heart skips a beat, wondering if what he's sensing could possibly be true. Gabe feels as if he's floating off his seat and grabs the end of the table, hanging on. "Somehow that little girl makes me want to be a better man." He shakes his head. "I don't know what it is, but every time I'm around her I think that I just need to be a good, good man for her."

"And you are."

An hour into their conversation, he realizes he's barely touched his food. Amy's plate is nearly full as well. If Gabe has to order three more meals in order to hold on to this table and this moment with Amy, he'll do it!

"I'm going to be a foster mom," she says. He sets his fork down, listening. "I was really nervous about it but I just kept feeling this nudge. Gloria says that a lot of people ignore the nudge."

"You've never ignored the nudge for anything. It's not in your DNA. Wow. A foster mom. Those will be some blessed kids!"

They order dessert and take their sweet time eating; the restaurant empties with the exception of a few employees sweeping the floor, filling salt and pepper shakers, and clunking around in the kitchen. When the waitress informs them that she needs to cash out for the evening, they laugh, realizing they have single-handedly shut the place down. A wintry cold blast of air hits their faces as Gabe opens the door and they step out onto the sidewalk. "You forgot the stuff for Gloria," he says, reaching back to reopen the door.

"You need to know something, Gabe." She looks at the star on top of the gazebo and smiles, surprised at herself for this. "I told you that I was no longer engaged but I didn't tell you why." She looks back at him and his eyes are full of questions. "He was a good guy but when it came time to set the wedding date I couldn't do it."

He waits for her to finish but she doesn't. "Why?"

"Because he wasn't you." Gabe is silent, not quite believing what he's hearing. "The truth is, I didn't come here to pick something up for Gloria. I was driving through town to go home when I saw your truck and I drove around the square three times just trying to drive on past. On the third time around, I said to myself that if there was a space open next to your truck, I would go inside and look for you. But if there wasn't a space I would drive home."

"And there was an open space next to my truck?" he says, craning his neck to see where he parked.

She shakes her head. "No." His mouth opens, listening. "I thought, that's a really stupid way to determine what could possibly happen in your future."

The wind picks up, blowing across their faces, but Gabe doesn't seem to notice. "What are you saying?"

"I don't know. All I know is that I don't

know. But I don't want to turn my back on a friendship or . . ."

He leans into her, kissing her once, before pulling back to look at her face. "I'm sorry. I was following a nudge."

She puts her hand on his cheek, and steps closer, kissing him, and then pulls away. "Me too."

"Remember when Ben came into Betty's after the Glory's Place fund-raiser?"

She sighs. "How could I forget!"

"He was right. I don't know how he knew it but he was right. I do love you." Her face is serious as she listens. "I never thought I'd see you again but I never stopped loving you, Amy." She turns her head, not sure if she's ready for this. "You told me the truth and I feel like I need to tell you the truth." She faces him again. "I never did. I never stopped." She shakes her head. "Please don't let that scare you away."

"I don't think it does. Maybe I'll be scared tomorrow when I remember everything that's been said, but right now I don't think I am."

He walks her to her car and she unlocks it, looking across the street to the gazebo and the star. "It's beautiful, isn't it?" Amy says.

"Maddie says it's a sign."

She looks at him. "A sign for what?"

"For us."

TWENTY-ONE

Gloria opens the door for Lauren and Travis, ushering them into her home. "I'm so sorry to bother you and Marshall at night," Lauren says.

"Oh my word! You would never be bothering us. Marshall isn't home from the store anyway. Even if he was, he would love to see both of your faces." She takes their jackets and hangs them on the hall tree in the entryway.

"Is Miriam coming?"

Gloria leads them into the living room, indicating that they should seat themselves on the sofa. "She should be here any minute. I called her as soon as you and I hung up."

Lauren sighs. "That gives me a second to tell you what happened before she gets here." The door opens and Lauren groans, resting her head on the back of the sofa. "Too late."

Miriam races into the living room, looking wide-eyed at all of them. "What's happened? What's wrong?"

Gloria puts her hands on the back of Miriam's shoulders and leads her to a chair. "Sit down, Miriam. And why do you think anything's wrong? Why is that always your first assumption?"

Miriam lifts her arm toward a window. "It's dark outside, Gloria. If this is good news, it would have been shared during the daylight hours. People only show up at your doorstep at night when they have bad news. That's been scientifically proven."

Gloria rolls her eyes and exhales. "That is so illogical that I don't even know how to respond." Miriam opens her mouth but Gloria puts a finger in her face. "Just hush until further notice." She turns to look at Lauren. "Go ahead, babe."

"Well . . . I . . . picked up my wedding dress just a little while ago." She stops talking when Miriam jumps to her feet, clapping her hands.

"Oh! It *is* good news! Where is it? I'm so excited to see it!" She looks at Travis. "But why is he here? The groom should never see the dress before the wedding day."

"He hasn't seen it," Lauren says.

Miriam swipes her hand across her forehead. "Phew! I know that you both are making some unconventional choices for this wedding, but I'm so glad that you're keeping the mystery and the beauty of the dress a secret until that very special moment." Lauren looks at Travis and he gives her an awkward smile, raising his shoulders. "What does that mean?" Miriam says, pouncing as soon as she notices the look. "Why did you do that, Travis? Why did you smile like this?" she says, mimicking the look on his face.

"I . . . didn't know my face did that."

She points at him. "It did. Your face did do that and you just did it again! Did you see it, Gloria?" Gloria begins to answer, but Miriam is impatient. "Where is the dress? If you picked up the dress a few minutes ago then surely it's here, right? Or is it in your car? Did they do something wrong to the dress? Because if they did, you don't have to worry. I will take care of everything."

Lauren shakes her head. "No, Miriam. It's nothing like that. The dress is beautiful. It was even more beautiful when I picked it up than on the day you bought it."

"And?" Miriam says, standing in front of her and Travis.

"And I saw a woman over by the gazebo when I was walking to my car. And she . . ."

Miriam motions for her to hurry up already and spit it out. "What? What?"

"She and her mom and her sister were the ones who bought the star for the gazebo."

"Oh, how nice. What does that have to do with our . . . your dress?"

"Should we all have something to drink?" Gloria says. "I can make some coffee or I have some cider or —"

"No one wants anything to drink, Gloria! Do I look parched to you?"

"No. But you do look kind of crazy."

Miriam disregards her and faces Lauren. "Go on."

"Well, it turns out that I saw her and her mom on the day that Travis was putting the star on the gazebo. Then I saw them in the dress shop, the first time that I went in to pick it up, and I overheard that they were trying to find a wedding dress."

"How very odd that they would be looking for a wedding dress in a dress and formal wear shop!" Miriam says, making Travis smile in that awkward way again.

"Then I saw them again in Wilson's looking for a dress and I pieced things together and realized that they couldn't afford a dress."

Gloria's hand flies to her mouth and Miriam falls into her chair, her hand covering her forehead. "You didn't," she says.

"I couldn't get her and her mom out of my mind. After I picked up the dress I saw her over at the gazebo, alone. I went over and . . ."

"Oh, please say you didn't talk to her," Miriam says, ashen.

"I did talk to her." Miriam lets out a small, guttural noise that makes Gloria reach for a magazine off the coffee table and begin to fan her. "Her name is Mandy and she had planned a Christmas wedding because her dad loved Christmas. In October he had the idea of getting the star for the gazebo, so that everyone in town could enjoy it. Then he was diagnosed with cancer and died only eleven days later. I just couldn't imagine it." She looks at Gloria, whose eyes have misted over, and says, "Gloria, you always say to hold things loosely, and as I was standing there talking to her, I realized that I didn't have a tight grip on that dress. But I do have a tight grip on all of you, and you're what matters most to me."

Gloria lays down the magazine and walks to the sofa, sitting next to Lauren, wrapping her in her arms. "I am so proud of you!" She leans back, putting her hands on Lauren's. "I just can't imagine what that one act of kindness is going to do for that woman for the rest of her life. She'll never forget it. And neither will I." She hugs Lauren again and then reaches over, patting Travis's leg. "Quite the woman you have here."

"I know," he says.

Miriam clears her throat and the three of them slowly look her way.

"Travis and I have already talked about it on the way over here, Miriam, and it might take some time, but we will pay you back for the dress. Every penny!"

Miriam makes a high-pitched noise that reaches the ceiling. "You will do no such thing. The dress was my gift to you, meaning that you were the owner of the dress, and could do with it whatever you wanted."

Lauren stands and moves to Miriam, who rises to give her a hug. "I love you so much, Miriam."

Miriam's eyes fill at the words and she clears her throat. "I know you do." She dabs at her eyes before anyone can see, and pats Lauren on the back. "With or without a dress, you'll still be the most beautiful bride that Grandon has ever seen." She and Gloria walk them to the door and Gloria sighs as she closes it behind them.

"That was quite the brave face you showed, Miriam," she says, leading her into the kitchen, where she uncovers a chocolate pie. She opens a cabinet and pulls down two plates, putting a slice of pie on each, before putting a kettle of water on to boil for tea.

Miriam sits at the kitchen table and puts her head down on it. "She gave it away. That beautiful, expensive dress. Gone."

Gloria sets the piece of chocolate pie in front of her. "But somehow, when she wrapped her arms around you and told you that she loves you, you forgot all about the money."

Miriam twists up her face in attempt to hold back the tears and looks up at the ceiling. "Shut up, Gloria."

Gloria takes a bite of her pie. "And as much as you'd like to resist the idea, I think that if you were placed in the exact same circumstances, you would do the same thing."

Miriam uses her fork to attack the pie. "You are old and delusional." She reaches across the table and squeezes her friend's hand. They both howl as they eat what Miriam describes as the best chocolate pie she's ever put into her mouth.

TWENTY-TWO

Gloria takes Lauren's coat, hanging it on the hall tree, and then walks to the stairs of her home. "I've been thinking for the last couple of days," she says, leading her to the second floor. "When my first husband died, I was going through his things and found something from our wedding day. I thought I should get rid of it, because no one in my family wanted to use it, but for some reason I held on to it."

She walks into the bedroom at the end of the upstairs hall and opens the closet, pulling out something on a hanger, covered with a long garment bag. She removes the bag and holds up an ivory fifties-style straight skirt, which looks to reach mid-calf, with an ivory brocade jacket, dotted with pearls. "I wore this for my wedding." She looks at Lauren, smiling. "As you can see, I was thinner then." She examines the skirt and jacket. "I know it doesn't look like much, but if you think that you could use it, you're welcome to wear it for your wedding." She sees the look on Lauren's face and says, "I know, it looks old and —"

"No!" Lauren says, stepping closer to touch the fabric. "It's beautiful! I can't believe you'd let me wear this."

Gloria hands it to her. "Would you like to try it on?" Lauren nods and Gloria steps out of the room into Marshall's study, where she uses her finger to wipe dust from the lamp base, computer screen, and edge of the desk. She straightens books on the shelves, and turns pictures to just the right angle.

"Okay, Gloria," Lauren says a few minutes later, opening the door.

Gloria stands in the doorway and her face loses its expression. She shakes her head, entering. "I knew it was beautiful but after all this time I never imagined it would look like this." She reaches out to touch the jacket. "It looks like it was made for you." Her eyes mist over, taking in the jacket and skirt. "So many years ago," she says, examining the fabric. "My word! The threads in this have held up much better than I have!" Lauren laughs and Gloria shakes off the tears. "Such memories! I was just a child myself." She looks at her. "And so in love.

Much like you." A tear rolls down her cheek and she wipes it away.

"Gloria, I can't wear this."

"I'm not crying because you're going to wear it." She pats her face. "I'm crying because that's what old people do when they see a couple setting off on a journey of marriage together. When I look at this dress, it reminds me of how young and naïve I was. When I put this on that day, I thought that everything would come up roses from that day forward. Walt being out of work, the death of our parents, a runaway child being gone for years, sickness, standing at Walt's grave. None of it entered my mind that day. But I'd go through all of it again with Walt." She smiles, looking at her. "That's why old people cry at weddings. We know the road that's up ahead and what it takes to travel it, and are so happy that you have someone to travel it with. It's quite the ride!" She puts her hands on Lauren's shoulders. "What a beautiful bride you're going to be." Lauren leans into her, hugging her. "We can have Heddy take a look at it and bring this waist in a little bit and she can reinforce these little pearls so they won't fall off, and it looks like something will need to be done to the sleeves, then I can take it to Jenny at the dry cleaners for some TLC."

Lauren's eyes are wide with questions. "Did you tell Miriam about this?"

Gloria shakes her head. "No. As soon as Marshall left for the store, I called you."

"What will she think?"

"She'll think it's old and worn out and make some crack that likens its age to me. Then I'll make some cracks about the highfalutin words she uses and, in the end, she'll say that she loves it, and that you are beautiful in it."

"Are you going to tell her today or should I?"

Gloria cocks her head, looking at her. "Oh, let's just watch her stress over finding another dress for a couple of days. Watching Miriam squirm at Christmas is really one of the great joys of the season for me." Lauren laughs out loud as she and Gloria look in the mirror together.

Gabe and Maddie each work on creating a Christmas card at Beside Me that will be given to local police or firefighters. Penny, from Grandon Craftworks, is leading the group in how to make an origami Christmas tree for the front of each card.

Gabe works at folding a tiny piece of paper and groans, looking at it. "My fingers are too big for this. Something is going to have to change pretty radically in order for this to look like a tree."

Maddie giggles, looking over at it. "It looks like a doghouse."

He turns the card sideways, tilting his head. "You're right! I could write something like, 'Have a doggone good Christmas.' "

She shakes her head, giggling. "That's awful."

He studies it. "I can't give this to anyone, let alone a police officer. He might arrest me because it's so bad." He thinks. "It's so bad it's criminal."

"Just start over and give that one to me."

He hands it to her. "Here you go. Have a doggone good Christmas."

She rolls her eyes, setting it aside. "Mr. G.?"

"Yeah."

"Will you keep doing this with me?"

He looks at her. "You mean, being part of Beside Me?" She nods. "Absolutely!"

She looks down at her work. "I'm so glad you can. You're one of my favorite people."

His heart aches inside him a little as he reaches for more paper to begin his tree again. "What do you want for Christmas?"

"I'm still thinking about that."

"Still thinking about it? You told that bully

kid that you wanted a ring."

"Not anymore."

"Because of what he said?"

She shrugs. "Just don't want one anymore."

He glances at her without turning his
head. "When I was a kid I knew what I
wanted for Christmas months ahead of
time."

She shrugs. "Kids change."

"Okay. Well, what are you doing for
Christmas?"

"Me and Linda will be at her house. What
will you do?"

"Hmm. I don't know." He leans over,
whispering. "Between us, I was kind of hoping that maybe Amy would want to spend it
with me."

She slams down the card she's working on
and looks at him. "Do you mean that you
and Amy are . . ." She doesn't know how to
say it.

He smiles. "Maybe. I sure hope so."

She jumps up from her seat and hugs him.
"From the first time I saw her I wanted you
to marry her!"

He opens his mouth in surprise, pushing
her away to look at her. "Whoa, whoa,
whoa! Who said anything about marriage?"

She crosses her arms, smiling. "I just did.

I told you right from the beginning that I found the perfect woman for you. Remember?"

He nods. "She is perfect for me."

She puts her hands on each of his cheeks, pushing so hard that his mouth is misshapen. "Don't blow it this time!" He laughs and she slaps his cheeks with each breath. "I'm serious! Don't! Blow it! With her!"

"I won't! I won't!" he says, laughing.

She sits down, satisfied with herself. "That's what I want for Christmas." He raises an eyebrow. "I want you and Amy together for every Christmas."

Twenty-Three

Amy finishes washing the dishes in her kitchen and picks up stray books and TV remotes from the living room before heading to her bedroom to change. Her heart is thumping; she is so nervous, feeling like a teenager about to go on a first date. She picks out a black turtleneck with a flowing, sea-foam-green vest over it and a pair of jeans. She looks at herself in the bathroom mirror, examining the lines around her eyes and the beginning of gray-colored roots at the hairline above her ears. This face doesn't fit a first date, she thinks. When she was in college, she had dreams of starting her own business, getting married, and having children, with two dogs running over the yard that surrounded their home. The face looking back at her is lined here and there with reality and the wisdom that comes with falls along the way. The doorbell rings and she exhales, taking one final look in the mirror before turning off the bathroom light.

Gabe is on the front porch wearing a blue dress shirt with a tie, and a plaid wool sports jacket with black pants. She grabs her coat from the closet and opens the door, smiling. "I think I might be underdressed."

He beams, looking at her. "I think you look great."

She moves aside for him to come in. "Seriously. Am I underdressed?"

"Maybe just change the jeans."

She closes the door and throws her coat on the back of the sofa, while she moves back down the hall toward her bedroom. "I thought you said we'd go out for barbecue or something," she says from behind her closed door.

"I decided on *something* instead of barbecue," Gabe says, looking at pictures on top of the fireplace mantel. "Your mom and dad look really good." He picks up the picture for a closer look. "Is this your niece? Did she graduate?"

Amy emerges from her bedroom wearing a long, navy blue skirt and tall brown boots. "She graduated in May. My brother feels old now." She looks down at herself. "Is this better?"

He smiles. "Perfect. You look amazing."

She looks around, uncomfortable in her

own home. "I don't know why, but I'm so nervous. I was thinking before you got here that I'm not really prepared for first dates anymore."

He puts the photo back on the mantel. "Me neither. So let's not think of it that way." She tries to muster a smile as his eyes scan her home. "I love your house. You're a great decorator. You've always known how things should go together."

She looks at him and feels her throat tighten. "What if we don't go together, Gabe? What if this doesn't work again? What will we do then?"

He steps in front of her. "What if it does work?" He smiles at her. "What will we do then?" He kisses her forehead. "Maddie told me not to blow it with you and I'm going to take her advice."

She laughs out loud. "She said that? Really?"

He reaches for her coat on the back of the sofa. "Yes! She gave me strict orders not to blow it this time."

He drives to the lake on the outskirts of Grandon and parks in front of Ellery's Seafood and Steaks. Amy looks at the cedar shake building and reaches back into her memory, trying to recall when she was here last.

"Do you remember this place?" Gabe asks.

"I've eaten here but I don't remember when."

He parks his truck and turns off the engine. "I brought you here on our first date."

"Oh yeah." She looks at him. "That wasn't our best night. Not a great first date. I complained too much and you drank too much and I had to drive you home."

"We were younger then and I was an idiot." She laughs, shaking her head. "Tonight, let's show those young people from all those years ago how two people get to know each other."

Gabe had requested the table by the fireplace a couple of days ago and the hostess leads them there, where he pulls Amy's chair out for her. He sits across from her, putting the napkin on his lap. "Did I tell you that you look amazing?"

"Yes. You did," she says, smiling. "And you look very handsome, Gabe. I actually think you've grown more handsome over the years."

"So my mother was right! I thought it was just a mom thing."

"How are your mom and dad?" she says, chuckling.

"They're doing great. I told them that I

was coming here with you tonight and I think my mom actually fainted." She laughs again and he talks over the laughter. "It was either that or she was standing on the other end of the phone with her mouth open, speechless." He mimics what his mother must have looked like. "They thought the world of you. It was very hard on them when we divorced, on my mom especially. And my dad thought you were supercool because you could carry on a conversation with him in Spanish."

"Only near the end of our marriage. And then it was so slow and painful. I don't remember much at all anymore."

He speaks slowly in Spanish and she looks down at the table, listening. She cocks her head and he says it one more time. "Well?"

She grins. "I heard the words *Spanish* and *bike.*"

He speaks in Spanish again and her eyes light up. "I can't pick out all of the words but you basically said, Spanish will come back to me like riding a bike."

"*Sí,*" he says.

The waiter comes and Amy finds herself beaming as Gabe orders filet mignon and she orders salmon. "Is this a special occasion?" he says to them.

Gabe looks at Amy and her eyes are warm.

"Yeah, it's our second date here."

When they finish their meal, Amy leans her arms on the table. "Will we do this again?"

"Would you like to do it again?" he says, hopeful.

Her mouth turns up a little as she nods. "I'd say this was a promising second date."

"Now what to do on the next date? George Bailey said he'd lasso the moon for Mary. I'm not sure I could swing that. I couldn't give you the world either. God's pretty much got the market closed there. I could —"

She shakes her head, smiling. "I've never wanted the world. I don't need fancy meals or fancy gifts. I've never gone for fancy anything. I just want to be with a man who —"

"Who knows your worth?" he asks.

"Yeah. And a man who —"

"Who sees that you are the most valuable thing on earth? A man who believes that the world is a better place with you in it and he can't imagine a world without you in it? Someone who feels like a better man when he's with you? A man who knew you when you were years younger but thinks you're more beautiful than ever? A man who doesn't look at magazine covers or on TV, the internet, or the movies for what a gorgeous woman looks like because none of them can hold a candle to you? A man who knows he can't live a day without you and wants the rest of his life to start with you as soon as possible?"

Tears pool in her eyes as she places her palms on the table, lifting herself up to kiss him.

Twenty-Four

Gabe carries a few groceries in his basket to the front at Clauson's and when he sees Ben, he slips out of the line he's standing in so he can receive one of Ben's notes. Each customer in front of him rummages through their bags as they exit and read notes like:

Christmas has to live in your heart. If it doesn't, it's just another day. Merry Christmas, Ben

Christmas really is the most wonderful time of the year! Hope it's wonderful for you, Ben

Scrooge said, "I will honor Christmas in my heart, and try to keep it all the year." That's good advice for all of us! Merry Christmas, Ben

As Gabe puts his groceries on the conveyor belt, he looks at Ben and smiles.

"Hello, Gabe," Ben says, reaching for the groceries.

"Hi, Ben! I moved over into this line so I can get one of your notes."

"I hear that people do that a lot," Ben says. The cashier nods, smiling in agreement. "How's Amy? You still love her, right?"

Gabe smiles as he pays. "I'd really like to know how you knew that."

Ben shrugs, handing him the two bags of groceries. "When you're around people as much as I am you become an expert." The cashier and Gabe laugh together. "You looked at Amy like my dad looks at my mom. Or how Travis looks at Lauren or how Mr. Marshall looks at Miss Glory. It was obvious," he says, reaching for the next customer's groceries.

Gabe pats Ben on the shoulder and says, "Have a great day, Ben. You sure make it awfully good for lots of other people."

He slides behind the steering wheel of his truck and sets the groceries on the passenger seat, reaching into one bag and then the other before finding the note. It's on a red piece of paper, shaped like a star, and reads, *Love came at Christmas and is here to stay. Merry Christmas, Ben.*

Gabe sticks the note inside his pocket and drives to Pender's Fine Jewelry on the town square, opposite Betty's and across the street from the library. Gabe zips up his coat as he gets out of his truck and runs inside the store. "Anything we can help you find?" a woman polishing a glass case asks.

"Looking for a ring," he says.

TWENTY-FIVE

Gabe and Amy pick Maddie up at Linda's house, promising to have her home no later than eight. She buckles herself in and crosses her arms, smiling. "What're you smiling at?" Gabe asks.

"I called it," she says.

Amy cocks her head. "Called what?"

"This," Maddie says, sweeping her arms out in front of her. "You two. Together. I called it."

Amy and Gabe laugh together and Amy reaches back to squeeze Maddie's leg.

"You did call it," Gabe says.

"And you're not blowing it, right?"

Gabe looks at Amy. "I don't know. Am I?"

Amy grins at Maddie. "I'm happy to report that he's not blowing it."

"Thanks to me," Maddie says, crossing her arms again. "So, where are we going?"

"It's a surprise," Gabe says, backing out of the driveway.

After they've driven several minutes and the sign for Carmine's comes into view, Maddie squeals in delight. "My favorite!"

"My favorite too," Amy says.

Ralph, the owner of Carmine's and a man probably around fifty-two or so with a slight build and receding hairline, leads them to a table and places menus in front of each of them. "The special today is Mama's Favorite."

"And what is Mama's Favorite?" Gabe asks.

"Spicy sausage, fresh mozzarella, ricotta, and pecorino romano cheeses, and spinach," Ralph says as he moves away from the table to seat other customers.

"Is Ralph the owner?" Maddie says, studying him as he helps at another table.

"He is," Gabe answers.

"Then why is this place called Carmine's?"

Gabe grins. "Let's just say Ralph is a genius at marketing and advertising." He sets his menu down. "And even though he's from somewhere in Kansas, he sure knows how to make a great Italian pizza."

"Mama's Favorite?" Amy says.

"She still knows me," he says, winking at Maddie.

"A slice of cheese for me," Maddie says.

Gabe raps his knuckles on the table. "You know what we need to do? We need to go ice-skating sometime."

Maddie grimaces at the thought. "I can't ice-skate."

"Have you ever gone ice-skating?" Gabe asks.

"No!"

"Then how do you know you can't do it?"

She looks at him as if to say it should be obvious. "I know what I can't do."

Amy glances over at Gabe. "One of my favorite memories as a child is ice-skating not too far from here with my family."

"Bet you didn't fall a few times," Maddie says.

"You're right. I didn't. I fell a bunch of times." Maddie glances up at her. "Too many times to count. The first time I put on a pair of ice skates I probably fell fifty times. I even sprained my ankle one time when I went. Everybody falls. Expect it. It's part of the fun."

Maddie spins her napkin on the table. "A grown-up's idea of fun stinks."

Gabe places their order with a waitress and then folds his arms on top of the table. "It is fun! We can take you to other fun spots around here too."

"Like where?"

Amy cocks her head, thinking, before saying, "Pumpkin Fest at Granger Farm, a trip to the falls, which are beautiful in the summer, uh . . ."

Gabe joins in with great enthusiasm. "The firefighters' chili cook-off and then the policemen's barbecue cook-off and the Humane Association's cookie bake-off."

"You only know food events," Amy says.

"I love food!"

Maddie laughs, listening to them. "I love you guys. I hope we'll always be friends."

Gabe and Amy look at each other and Amy puts her arm around Maddie's shoulders. "We will be." She clears her throat and reaches for her water. "So, what are you wearing to Lauren's wedding?"

Maddie shrugs. "Beats me."

"Do you have a pretty dress or a skirt or a pair of dressy slacks?"

She bulges out her eyes. "No way."

"Then we need to make a stop at Wilson's. Every little girl needs something to wear to a dress-up occasion. Don't you agree, Gabe?"

"Yes, I do! But first we eat," he says, lifting his fork in the air.

When they finish eating, they bundle up and brace against the cold for the short walk around the square to Wilson's. Maddie holds on to Gabe's and Amy's arms and shrieks whenever the wind whips up around them.

"Hi, Mr. Marshall," Maddie says on entering the store. Marshall Wilson is chatting with a sales clerk but his face brightens on seeing Maddie. "These are my friends Gabe and Amy. Amy helps at Glory's Place." She looks at Amy. "This is Miss Glory's husband."

Amy extends her hand. "I just love your wife."

"That makes two of us."

"Three of us," Maddie says, thrusting her finger upward.

"Are you looking for anything in particular?" Marshall says, looking down at the little girl.

"They're making me get something fancy for Lauren's wedding."

Marshall nods, smiling. "Ah. Well, it just so happens that we have lots of things that are just fancy enough for adults, yet not so fancy for little girls, and all can agree on. Just head downstairs and ask for Mary Beth. Tell her I said you're looking for something fancy but not so fancy." He bends down to whisper in her ear. "And be sure you pick up some hot chocolate and the cookie of the day. It's a pinwheel with lots of sprin-kles."

Maddie smiles as they make their way downstairs. Mary Beth proves invaluable, first picking out a pair of fake-velvet pants with a beautiful turtleneck, then a dress with a black velvet top and a red satin bot-tom, and a long black skirt with a fun, frilly top. Gabe and Amy wait as Maddie tries on each outfit and then twirls and spins in front of them. The more they compliment her, the more she giggles and the more they smile. Always conscious of her leg, Gabe and Amy both assume that she would choose the pants and are surprised when she chooses the black skirt and frilly top. "I've never had anything like this," Maddie says, touching the blouse.

"Well, you can't wear a skirt like that without boots in this kind of weather," Gabe says.

A simple pair of black dress boots is chosen, and as they walk to the cash register Gabe and Amy notice Maddie beaming, looking at the clothes in her arms. "Lau-ren's wedding is going to be the best day of my life," she says, placing the clothes in front of the cashier.

Gabe carries Maddie's bags to the front door of Linda's house and hands them over to Maddie as she goes inside. Before Linda can close the door, Maddie wraps her arms around him, burying her head against his chest. "Thank you so much, Mr. G." Linda smiles as Gabe waves good-bye.

Amy is quiet when Gabe gets back in the truck. "Anything wrong?" he asks.

"I just watched her hug you. She's so excited over those clothes." She looks over at him. "I really love that little girl."

TWENTY-SIX

At eleven thirty on the morning of the wedding the sun is so bright against the snow that many in the setup crew wear sunglasses, while others squint as they place chairs around the gazebo. Miriam's arm swings around, directing the position of each chair, making sure the placement is perfect, while looking down at her phone in the other hand.

"Why do you keep looking down at that phone?" Gloria scolds. "It's annoying."

"I'm watching the weather forecast, Gloria!"

"It's cold this morning. It will be cold this afternoon. There's your forecast," Gloria says, snatching the phone out of her hand. "You won't melt during the wedding ceremony."

"Melting is not my concern. Turning into a Popsicle is!"

"Popsicles are sweet, Miriam. Trust me,

you're not in danger."

"I want the day to be beautiful, Gloria. Lauren deserves a beautiful wedding day."

Gloria sighs, handing Miriam's phone back to her. "It'll be cold but it will be beautiful. Everything will be perfect for her."

Heddy is still busy working on Lauren's wedding ensemble in Stacy's living room, while two hairdressers work on Lauren's and Stacy's hair. "Heddy," Lauren says, under curlers. "It's beautiful. You don't need to keep working on it."

Heddy bends over her work, carefully sewing on more pearls to the new sleeves she created because the original sleeves were torn in a couple of spots. "It's not perfect yet. But it will be!"

"Are you going to have time to get ready yourself?"

Heddy keeps her head down, shaking it. "Doesn't matter. Nobody will be looking at me anyway."

"Or me!" Stacy says.

"I'll look at you, Mom," Ben says from the kitchen.

The women burst into laughter. "What in the world is Travis doing right now?" Lauren wonders out loud.

"Watching TV while eating a bowl of

cereal in his boxers," Stacy says.

"Dalton went target shooting with his groomsmen on the morning of our wedding and barely made it there on time," Heddy says to the sleeve. "I was ready to kill that man right on our very own wedding day!"

The women cackle and Ben peers around the corner to see what all the noise is about. He shrugs and heads back to his sandwich in the kitchen.

"Were you nervous, Stacy?" Lauren asks as the hairdresser begins to unroll a curler.

"Of course."

"Were you nervous, Heddy?"

"I was getting married in front of Dalton's mother. That woman would have made the president nervous." She looks up from her work. "If you feel it, it's normal. But you just remember that everybody at your wedding loves you and Travis. Nobody there could scare the president."

"I think Miriam could," Stacy says, snorting. They cackle louder together and Ben sticks his head around the corner once again before sneaking off to find the safety of his dad.

Gloria and Miriam glance up from their work at the gazebo as Dalton honks his car horn, pulling in to a spot. He's shaking his head as he steps from the vehicle.

"Why does Dalton's face look like that, Gloria? What's wrong?"

"Nothing's wrong. His face is fine. He's fine. I'm sure he's fine," Gloria says, hoping it's true.

"We've got problems," Dalton says when he's close enough for them to hear.

"I knew it," Miriam says. "Your horrible face, Dalton!"

He looks stricken. "What's wrong with my face?"

Miriam throws her arms in the air. "Why do I listen to you, Gloria?"

Gloria ignores her. "What's wrong, Dalton?"

He stops in front of them. "The heat is out at Glory's Place." Miriam groans, throwing her arms higher in the air. He holds his hand out to calm her. "I've had a couple of guys there for the last hour trying to get it running again. I was hoping to get it taken care of so that it wouldn't ruin your morning."

"By the look on your face I'm assuming that you have come in person to ruin our morning?" Miriam says.

He nods. "They need a part and of course they can't get it until late this afternoon or possibly tomorrow morning."

"So we'll freeze at the wedding *and* the reception! A perfect day, right, Gloria?" Miriam says, her voice icy with sarcasm.

"Well, thankfully it broke down on the first day of Christmas break and the children are all expected to come to the wedding, so we don't need to use the building."

"The reception, Gloria!" Miriam says, exasperated. "The reception!"

"Would you hush up with that caterwaulin' so we can all think?!" Gloria snaps. She looks up into the sky. "How about Carmine's?"

"I already have all the food for the reception," Miriam says, her eyes huge like saucers. "If we went to Carmine's we'd have to buy greasy pizzas and eat off sticky plastic tablecloths. Besides, they're always swamped for dinner."

"Betty's?" Dalton offers.

Gloria shakes her head. "Betty told me on Monday that two of her girls are out with the flu. I couldn't throw this at her with her being shorthanded this week." She makes a clicking sound with her tongue. "How about Kirkland's on the Lake?"

Miriam moans. "They're booked months in advance, and again, we already have all the food!"

Gloria nods her head as if the perfect idea

has bolted down from heaven. "We'll have the reception at my house. Dalton, can you get the decorations moved to my house ASAP?"

"Gloria! Your house is the size of a bread box," Miriam says.

"Then everyone will be nice and cozy," Gloria says, thinking out loud. "Heddy's with Lauren and Stacy but call the rest of Stacy's family. Call my son. And call Amy. Maybe she can help." Dalton pulls out his phone and begins calling.

Miriam's hands haven't stopped fluttering since Dalton arrived. "You have wrapping paper and unwrapped presents everywhere, Gloria! And you left that cake mess in the kitchen and that ridiculous calendar! Oh, that's priceless hanging on the wall! Today it said, *It's colder than a well-digger's butt!* Who wants to read that at a wedding reception? Is your house even clean?"

Gloria puts a hand on her hip and squares off in front of Miriam. "It's not a laboratory like your home, Miriam, but it's not a toxic-waste dump either! You know what else my calendar says? It says, *The madder I get, the thicker my Southern accent gets!*" Her accent gets soupy thick. "So listen up! Either you zip the British snobbery and help make this day perfect for Lauren and Travis or it'll be a month of Sundays before you're welcome in my home again!"

Miriam's mouth hangs open for several moments before she begins to snicker; she and Gloria grasp each other's hands and laugh together. "Head to your house and I will finish here," Miriam says, wiping tears from her eyes. "I'll come just as soon as we finish." She squeezes Gloria's hand. "And the day will be beautiful *and* perfect!" Gloria wraps her up in one of those bear hugs she's famous for. "It's been a long time since you've thrown one of those hissy fits."

"Well, at least it wasn't a conniption fit," Gloria says, walking away.

"What does a conniption fit mean?"

"Run for your life!"

Twenty-Seven

At three fifteen, the final wedding guests arrive bundled up in winter coats, hats, gloves, and scarves, and Ben hands them each a blanket and ushers them to their seats. At three thirty, all eyes around the gazebo watch as Lauren, Stacy, and Dalton ride past them in a horse-drawn carriage before stopping in front of the gazebo. Dalton first helps Stacy to the ground before extending his hand to Lauren. Gloria's eyes fill at the sight of her. "Heddy! The skirt and jacket are just beautiful," she says, wiping her eyes. "You worked magic over that old fabric."

Heddy shakes her head. "I didn't do much. It's who wears it that makes it beautiful," she says, making Gloria smile through her tears, remembering the girl she was so many years ago, walking down a church aisle toward Walt.

Dalton crooks his arm for Lauren. "Travis is a blessed man," he says.

"Don't make me cry, Dalton. I'm wearing fake eyelashes and I don't know if they stay on through tears!"

He throws his head back, laughing. "They look beautiful. You look beautiful. Are you ready?" She nods and squeezes his arm as Stacy leads them, walking toward the gazebo. When Lauren sees Travis, her stomach flutters as he rocks back and forth on his feet. If it's cold, she doesn't notice. If the wind is blowing, she doesn't seem to mind. She reaches her hand out when she sees Gloria and Marshall, Miriam, and Heddy, and they reach for her, squeezing her arm or hand as she passes.

"You're stunning," Miriam says, her eyes gleaming.

"Just gorgeous," Gloria says, blowing her a kiss.

Stacy walks up the stairs of the gazebo and takes her place opposite Gabe, smiling at him. When Dalton and Lauren reach the top, she turns and waves at the children from Glory's Place, and Maddie and the other children wave and applaud. Maddie grabs hold of Amy's hand and they smile at Gabe, who looks striking in his dark suit.

"Who gives this woman away?" Pastor James asks.

"I am proud to say that I do, along with

her entire family at Glory's Place," Dalton says, leaning over to kiss Lauren's forehead. He walks her over to Travis and Travis steps beside her. "She's all yours, Travis. Take great care of her." Travis shakes his hand and Dalton pats him on the shoulder before taking his seat next to Heddy.

The kids from Glory's Place file out of their seats and line up on the gazebo stairs as the music to "When God Made You" begins to pour through the speakers. Lauren and Travis can't help smiling at the lyrics: *But now that I have found you I believe / That a miracle has come.*

Gabe catches Amy's eye and they smile. Gloria, Miriam, and Heddy each wipe their eyes, and as the children sing the chorus, tears fill Lauren's eyes.

The children wave at Lauren when the song finishes and she looks up, trying to keep the tears from falling and ruining her makeup. Pastor James speaks briefly before saying, "Lauren, a year ago this town took you in, but today I need to ask you, do you take this man to be your husband?"

She laughs and says, "I do!" loudly enough for all to hear.

When Lauren stumbled upon Grandon one year ago she never imagined this day. She never dreamed of people adopting her as one of their own or of having anyone in her life who would think of her as family. She never thought she could love anyone as she loves Travis or that anyone could love her in a way that makes her feel safe and complete. She never imagined that she could love her work and feel excited each morning as she faced a new day. The thought of God pulling her up out of her pit seemed impossible a year ago, but Gloria says that "pulling up and out" is easy for God. We just have to reach up. She's so grateful that she did reach up, and her smile stretches up to the sky as Travis squeezes her hand.

Gloria's house swells with guests. They have to find places to sit, on the fireplace hearth and even the stairs, but no one complains. The finger foods that Miriam had catered for the reception are a big hit and, thankfully, provide easy cleanup. She and Amy each stay busy walking through the house, acting as makeshift waitresses, refreshing drinks and taking dirty dishes.

"I'm so sorry you couldn't have your reception at Glory's Place," Gloria says, hugging Lauren.

"I've always loved your house, Miss Glory! I actually wanted to have it here but I just didn't have the nerve to ask you."

Gloria throws her arms over her head. "Are you kidding? You can ask me anything, anytime. As long as I have breath in my body I will do anything for you."

"Just be sure you stay on her good side and she doesn't throw a conniption fit," Miriam says, eavesdropping.

Lauren glances at Gloria, puzzled. "What does that mean?"

"Run for your life!" Miriam says, making Gloria laugh. Miriam holds on to Lauren's arm and directs Travis to stand next to her as she gathers the children from Glory's Place to the center of the floor. "Excuse me, everyone," she says, clapping her hands together. "Stacy has been working with the children on a surprise wedding gift for our happy couple."

Lauren's mouth opens wide as the children assemble in front of her and Travis. "What have you been up to?" she says, making them laugh.

Stacy directs Miriam to press play on the CD player and music for "I Got You Babe" fills the living room. The kids who remember, correctly use gestures to act out the song, while others are always a gesture or two behind, making Lauren and Travis smile. While Miriam switches CDs the children say in unison, "Congratulations, Lauren and Travis. We love you and will miss you while you're gone!"

"I'll miss you too," Lauren says.

"Gotta be honest," Travis says. "I won't." The guests laugh as music for the Monkees' "I'm a Believer" begins. Lauren and Travis begin to dance and the guests follow suit, turning Gloria's living room into a make-shift dance floor.

On the final note, Lauren raises her arms and yells, "That was the *best* wedding present ever!"

Miriam quiets the guests, saying, "It is time to present Mr. and Mrs. Mabrey as they have their first dance together as man and wife." Travis grabs Lauren's hands as people clear the "dance floor." Miriam pushes play on the CD recording of Garth Brooks singing "To Make You Feel My Love." Halfway through the song the children from Glory's Place begin to giggle.

"How long is this?" Jace says out loud.

"This is so boring!" Brianna says, her knees nearly buckling from the boredom of it all.

"Our songs were soooo much better," Evan says, rolling his eyes.

Travis and Lauren begin to laugh as the children comment one after the other about the length of the song, the sheer drudgery of watching two people slow dance, and how one child's pants are too tight and he's ready to go home.

"When do we get to dance with her?" Luke asks, tapping Travis on the back. "You said she'd come back to us, remember?"

Travis looks over his shoulder at him. "I thought I'd at least have her to myself this one day." The guests boom with laughter as Luke shakes his head and steps in to dance with Lauren. Not to be left alone, Travis reaches for Maddie's hand and lifts her up to finish the dance with him.

"You are bringing her back, right, Mr. T.?" Maddie asks as he dances her around the living room.

"Don't you worry about that," he says. "There's no way I could keep Lauren away from you kids."

Miriam plays upbeat music so all the kids can dance with Travis and Lauren, and Amy rests her head on Gabe's shoulder, watching them. "What a difference a year can make in somebody's life," she says.

"A year?" Gabe says. "What a difference a few weeks make!" He kisses her forehead and steps to Maddie, bowing to ask for a dance. He lifts her onto his feet and dances her around the room as Amy watches, beaming. This reception is perfectly loud and boisterous and the opposite of what Miriam had in mind, but she also can't help smiling as she watches.

To Miriam's dismay, during the cutting of the cake, the bride and groom each shove cake pieces in the other's face, making her grimace and the guests cheer, but she's ready with hand wipes to clean up the mess so the cake can be cut up and distributed to the guests according to her time chart of events.

Two hours later, many of the guests leave before Lauren and Travis open their gifts. The generosity begins to overwhelm Lauren and she waves her hand in front of her face, attempting to hold back the tears. "You didn't have much on your wedding registry at the store," Marshall says. "So I had Judy and some of the other women at the store beef it up with everything you need to start a home. And I'm happy to report that everything was purchased."

"I don't know what . . ." She stops, looking at the boxed set of dishes in her hand. "You didn't have to do . . ."

"We wanted to, babe," Gloria says.

Lauren begins to cry and Dalton yells out, "Watch out, everybody! She's got fake eyelashes on!" Lauren throws a wad of wrapping paper at him.

As the music, food, and party continue, Gabe and Travis carry the gifts upstairs to keep in Gloria's spare room until Travis and Lauren return from their honeymoon. As they stack the last of the gifts on the floor, Gabe realizes that the time is nearing for Travis and Lauren to leave and he extends his hand. "Congratulations again! You both will be very happy."

"And so will you," Travis says. Gabe isn't following him. "You and Amy." Gabe shifts on his feet, sticking his hands inside his pockets. "I see it, Gabe. Everybody sees it. You love her."

Gabe smiles. "I know."

"And she loves you."

Gabe nods. "She does. I never thought it could happen again. But she does." They walk out of the bedroom and keep their voices low as they walk down the stairs, where Amy and Maddie are looking up at them. Travis turns to whisper something to Gabe and Amy notices a small smile lift Gabe's face.

"What was that all about?" she asks when he reaches the bottom step.

"We just finished taking the gifts up to the room," Gabe says.

"What was Travis whispering? Are you two

up to something?"

Maddie looks up at Gabe, raising an eyebrow. "Yeah, what were you whispering? I'm never allowed to whisper in class. It's rude."

"Maybe it's a secret and we're not supposed to know," Amy says to Maddie.

"A secret?" Miriam says, gathering dishes from the living room. "Tell me! I love secrets."

"We can't tell you," Maddie says. "It's Mr. G.'s secret."

Travis watches Gabe's face and laughs. "You started this!" Gabe says, shaking his head.

"What did he start?" Lauren says, walking near to hug Travis from behind.

"That's what we're trying to find out," Miriam says. "It appears a mystery surrounds your husband and Gabe."

The room has grown smaller as Gloria and Marshall, Dalton and Heddy, Stacy and her family, Gabe's parents, and others gather close. "What's happening?" Gloria asks.

"That's what we're trying to find out," Miriam says. "Whatever it is, it's not on my time chart!"

Travis bends forward, chuckling, almost sorry that he has put Gabe in this position.

"Sorry, everybody. I just made an observation and said something off-the-cuff to Gabe. I didn't mean to get him in hot water."

"What did you say?" Lauren asks.

Travis looks at Gabe, wondering if he has permission to say it, but Gabe's eyes are on the floor.

Gabe waves his hand to keep Travis from saying anything else. He looks at Amy. "He said, 'What are you waiting for? You know you want Amy as your wife. Why don't you ask her?' "

Twenty-Eight

Amy gasps as Gabe reaches for her hand and Maddie's eyes widen. "I'm not worthy to have you as my wife again, Amy. I know that. I'm not worthy of the happiness you bring me, or worthy of the way you make me feel by just entering a room that I'm in. I don't deserve your forgiveness, but somehow I'm standing here with the possibility of you in my life forever and I can only see that as God's favor." Tears flow over Amy's hand and she laughs as Gabe gets down on one knee. "Amy Denison, I'm not the man I was. I hope you know that." She nods, laughing through the tears. "And I promise you that I will try to be a better man every day of my life with you. I promise that I will be the husband you've prayed for." He pauses and she puts her other hand on top of his. "Would you be my wife again?"

Amy can't find her voice but nods her head, pulling him up to kiss him. "Yes!" she says, over the cheers and applause. "Yes, I will!" She kisses him again and Maddie hugs them.

"Bet this wasn't on your time chart," Gloria says to Miriam, leaning over to see the chart in her hand. Miriam tosses it over her shoulder, making both of them laugh.

Gabe's parents are the first to break through the small crowd to throw their arms around Gabe and Amy. Gabe's mother's face is wet as she says, "We always loved you, Amy!" Her words are tumbling out so fast that Gabe puts his arm around her shoulder, kissing her cheek.

"Hold on, Aunt Molly!" Travis yells above the cheers and Gabe's mom's wailing. "When's the date?"

"Whenever she tells me," Gabe says.

"Why not now?" Travis says, looking at everyone. Gabe opens his mouth but Travis isn't finished. "Everybody you love is here. Nearly everybody. We can call Amy's parents and get them over here. And everybody's dressed for a wedding."

"And there's plenty of food," Miriam says, stepping forward in her role as wedding planner.

"And the minister's still here," Pastor James says, smiling from the back of the living room. "You can get the official paperwork tomorrow."

Gabe looks at Amy and she looks down at Maddie, who has her arms wrapped around her waist. "This isn't the time. This is Travis and Lauren's day."

"We've had our day," Lauren says. "And it was the best day of my life. If you get married it will make it amazing!"

Amy smiles, hugging her, and shakes her head, looking at Gabe. "Are you sure?"

"Yes, he's sure!" Maddie says.

"Are *you* sure?" Gabe asks Amy.

Amy nods. "I'm positive." She can't believe this. "Can I at least dry my face and call my parents?"

Miriam races over to her. "Go right up the stairs and we will get you ready."

"I need my phone," Amy says, trying to remember where she put her purse.

"I'll call your parents," Gabe says. "I already talked to them a few days ago."

Amy stops. "When?"

"I went over to their house and we had a five-hour chat. I told them I loved you and wanted to marry you and asked for their blessing. Of course I didn't know then that it would happen this quickly! I assumed there'd be months of planning ahead of us. You actually called your mom while I was there. She said she was just going to lie down because she had a headache."

"She lied to me?"

He nods. "She had to. You were being very pushy about bringing a pizza over that night."

"They had asked me to come over for dinner and I was being helpful! So you asked for their blessing and . . ."

"And if they pick up the phone when I call them right now I'm sure they'll come over. It didn't hurt that you had already put in a good word for me with them." He smiles. "Your mom said that you told them that you adored me."

Amy puts her hand on Gabe's face. "You are a crazy man and I do adore you." She begins to laugh as Maddie grabs her hand, leading her upstairs with Miriam, Gloria, and Lauren.

Amy's parents arrive just minutes after Gabe's phone call and they hug Gabe's parents in a minireunion. Amy's mom, Theresa, is wearing black pants with a red sweater and Amy's dad, Jay, is in black slacks with a buttondown shirt and tie. "I refused to come to my daughter's wedding wearing sweatpants and I insisted that Jay take off his football jersey!" Theresa says.

There's no time for them to see Amy as

Miriam hurries down the stairs explaining, "We need to hurry things along so that Travis and Lauren can get to the airport in time to catch the plane for their honeymoon."

The living room booms with chatter and laughter, and Heddy hurries to the piano, playing "Joy to the World," as Pastor James shows Gabe and Travis where to stand. When Miriam waves at her, Heddy begins the wedding march and Maddie leads Amy down the stairs. Amy's hair has been swept up and she's wearing the same red dress she had on for Lauren and Travis's wedding but with one of Miriam's cream-colored silk scarves, which tumbles over the back of her shoulders, nearly reaching the floor, and is clipped in place with one of Gloria's brooches with tiny blue gems. "Something old *and* blue," Gloria said when she pinned it in place.

Amy carries Stacy's matron-of-honor flowers and hands them to Maddie when her dad steps through the crowd to reach for her hand, kissing her cheek as he does so. Pastor James smiles as they take their places in front of him. "I've never said this twice in one day but . . . Who gives this woman away?"

Amy's dad says, "Her mother and I," on

top of the laughter.

"Gabe and Amy have asked to say their own vows. Since this was spontaneous, there are no rings but they'll —"

"Here!" Maddie says, waving her arm in the air with the bracelets that Gabe and Amy gave her a few weeks ago. "You can use these!" Gabe and Amy smile as she removes them from her arm.

"Well, then," Pastor James says. "Do you have the wedding bracelets, Maddie?" Her face widens in a smile as she hands one to Gabe.

Gabe holds the bracelet in his palm in front of him. "I'm so honored that you have agreed to be my wife, Amy. We got these bracelets many years ago because they're made with a cord of three strands. It was supposed to be God and us together. Remember? A cord of three that can't be broken. But I never let God in and pushed you away, leaving a cord of one, and I was a weak cord." She smiles, looking at him. "I promise to keep you and God in this cord of three this time. I promise to love you and cherish you and be faithful to you and believe in you for the rest of my life. I promise to protect you and defend you and make you laugh for the rest of my life." Amy laughs as her eyes fill with tears. Gabe continues. "I promise to be true and faithful to you and love you well. I'm still flawed and far from perfect but I promise to be a husband the right way this time." He slips the bracelet onto her wrist and Amy opens her palm for Maddie to give her Gabe's bracelet.

"Gabe Rodriguez, I take you as my husband because I believe in miracles. I see a miracle when I see the man that you've become. I believe in miracles when I think of all that was wrong with us the first time we tried this, and I see all that is good with us this time. We're in the same bodies but we're not the same people. God still makes all things new, doesn't He? I had a hard time believing that before but I do now." Watery eyes fill the living room and Gloria rests her head on Marshall's shoulder, wiping a tear and smiling at Miriam. What a day this has been! Amy clears her throat as she puts the bracelet on Gabe's wrist. "I promise to encourage you and help you and believe in you, being faithful to you only, because you have always been and will always be the man of my dreams."

Pastor James waits a moment to make sure they're through with their vows and looks at Gabe, opening his mouth to speak, but Gabe raises his hand, looking at Amy. She smiles and nods at him, squeezing Maddie's hand. He bends down on one knee in front of Maddie and pulls a small box from his pocket. "Maddie, I ordered this from the jeweler and picked it up just this morning." Her eyes widen in surprise. "You told some kid at school that you wanted a ring for Christmas but he didn't think you deserved a ring. I think you deserve the most beautiful jewels in the world. When I ordered it, I thought this would just be a ring from ole Mr. G., but Amy and I talked a few minutes ago and we don't think it's just a Christmas gift that I give you. We're hoping that with this ring you'll take us to be your parents." Maddie begins to cry and audible gasps are heard in the living room. "I'd love to be your dad, Maddie."

Amy kneels down beside him. "And I'd love to be your mom."

"If you'll have us," Gabe says.

Maddie crumples into them, and when she's able to speak, she pulls away, looking at them. "Yes!" The living room erupts with applause as Gabe puts the ring on Maddie's finger, hugging her. "So, should I call you Dad or Mr. G. in school?"

"Whatever's cool with you," Gabe says. "I know that having your dad work at the school might not be so cool."

She bobs her head up and down, grinning. "Oh! I think it'll be really cool!"

"With the power vested in me," Pastor James says, "I now pronounce you man and wife. Kiss your family, Gabe!"

TWENTY-NINE

Travis and Lauren are the first to congratu-
late them and they give quick hugs and wave
as they run for the door. Lauren brings
Gloria, Miriam, Dalton, Heddy, Stacy, and
her son Ben into a group hug. "I love you
all," she says, her voice breaking.

"Go on now," Gloria says, kissing the top
of her head.

"Get to Florida and thaw out," Miriam
says, tears rimming her eyes.

The door closes behind Travis and Lauren, and then Gloria, Miriam, Dalton,
Heddy, and Stacy look at one another, each
of them misty-eyed, and they begin to laugh
at the sight of one another.

Gloria bends down to hug Maddie and
her voice catches as she says, "All I can say
is, Merry Christmas, Maddie! I'm so happy
for all of you!"

"So when do we all get to live together?"

Maddie says, reaching for Gabe's and Amy's hands.

"I'll call Patricia Anderson first thing tomorrow morning," Amy says.

"Can you ask that lady if Linda can be my grandma?"

"The only one we need to ask about that is Linda and I'm absolutely, positively sure that she will say yes!" Amy says.

"This has been the best Christmas holiday ever!" Gloria says.

Miriam throws her arms into the air. "You say that every year, Gloria!"

Gloria turns to her. "And am I right this year?"

Miriam smirks, defeated. "Yes. You are."

"Miriam agrees with me. It's a Christmas miracle!" Gloria says, making the room laugh.

"You simply must take your first dance together," Miriam says, reaching for the CD with the song titled "When God Made You" from Lauren and Travis's ceremony. Gabe takes his wife's hand and leads her to the center of the living room, where they begin to dance, but somewhere in the middle of the song, Gabe kisses her and never stops, making Maddie close her eyes.

"Yuck! Are they always going to do this?" she says, covering her eyes.

"I'm afraid so," Gloria says, squeezing Maddie's shoulders.

After pictures are taken and much chatter, Gloria takes Maddie by the hand. "Since none of us were prepared for this joyous event," she says, patting the small hand in hers, "once the lovebirds return from their honeymoon, we will throw you a wedding/adoption party! How does that sound?"

"Who will be in charge?" Miriam asks.

Gloria shakes her head. "You will, O Queen!" Miriam nods her head, satisfied.

Gabe reaches for Amy's hand, talking to everyone left in the room. "I still can't believe we're married again." He looks at Amy and she smiles, not quite believing it's real either. "We need to get Maddie back to Linda's and let her know what happened tonight and then we need to get home and plan our honeymoon." He looks at Amy. "Are you ready to go home, Mrs. Rodriguez?"

"I am, Mr. Rodriguez." He kisses her and feels Maddie patting his side.

"Come on, already!"

He looks down at her. "Get used to it. You'll be seeing this all the time!"

Maddie sighs. "That's what I hear!"

It's a cold but sunny day in January when Gabe and Amy, Maddie, her longtime foster mom, Linda, Patricia Anderson, Travis and Lauren, Gloria, Miriam, Dalton and Heddy, and Gabe's and Amy's parents arrive at the courthouse with balloons and streamers. Judge Marlene Dane says that this is her favorite part of her job as she declares Maddie's adoption as legal to shouts and cheers.

Gabe lifts Maddie and squeezes her. "I love you, sweet girl," he says, kissing her head.

"You're my dad now?"

"I'm afraid so. The judge made it legal."

"And Amy's my mom?"

"That's the deal," Amy says.

"So, just like that, it's all over?"

Gabe shakes his head. "Nope. Just like that, it's all beginning."

ABOUT THE AUTHOR

Donna VanLiere is the *New York Times* and *USA Today* bestselling author of *The Good Dream, Finding Grace, The Angels of Morgan Hill,* and many Christmas books, including the perennial favorites *The Christmas Shoes* and *The Christmas Hope.* She travels as a speaker and lives in Franklin, Tennessee, with her husband and three children.

The employees of Thorndike Press hope you have enjoyed this Large Print book. All our Thorndike, Wheeler, and Kennebec Large Print titles are designed for easy reading, and all our books are made to last. Other Thorndike Press Large Print books are available at your library, through selected bookstores, or directly from us.

For information about titles, please call:
(800) 223-1244

or visit our website at:
gale.com/thorndike

To share your comments, please write:
Publisher
Thorndike Press
10 Water St., Suite 310
Waterville, ME 04901